TRADING FUTURES

Matthew Oxenhay is a stranger to his wife, an embarrassment to his children, and a failed contender for the top job at his City firm. Seizing on his sixtieth birthday party as an opportunity to deliver some rather crushing home truths to his assembled loved ones, it seems as though he may have hit rock bottom. The reality, however, is that he has some way to go yet ... Matthew unpicks the threads that bind him: the suburban home, the City career, the life so different to what he once imagined. When he unexpectedly bumps into Anna — the one who got away — the stage is set for an epic unravelling.

Books by Jim Powell
Published by Ulverscroft:

THE BREAKING OF EGGS

JIM POWELL

◆

TRADING FUTURES

Complete and Unabridged

ULVERSCROFT
Leicester

First published in Great Britain in 2016 by
Picador
an imprint of
Pan Macmillan
London

First Large Print Edition
published 2016
by arrangement with
Pan Macmillan
London

A catalogue record for this book is available
from the British Library.

ISBN 978–1–4448–3050–7

Published by
F. A. Thorpe (Publishing)
Anstey, Leicestershire

Set by Words & Graphics Ltd.
Anstey, Leicestershire
Printed and bound in Great Britain by
T. J. International Ltd., Padstow, Cornwall

This book is printed on acid-free paper

For Kay

1

What I have decided to do is simple. It is cowardly. It is pathetic. But it is simple. I shall pull off the road and call home. If my wife has returned, and if she answers, I will say that my journey has been delayed, that I will be home at about eight p.m. If she has not returned, if she does not answer, I will turn the car round, go back to Somerset and stay there. Then I'll commence the divorce proceedings.

God, the A303 is a boring road. Is there any more boring road in England?

If the fifth car that passes me is white, I will stop and make the call. No, I'm not sure that's a good idea. Because if it isn't white, I'll have to start all over again and there's a limit to how many times I can count five cars without forgetting what number I've reached, and then I might find myself making the call when the fourth car is white, which wouldn't do at all. Let's just say I'll make the call quite soon.

Perhaps there are some more pills in the glove compartment. I could do with a few right now. There don't seem to be. Why do they still call it the glove compartment? Nobody wears gloves any more. Perhaps the people who design cars do. If it were up to me, I would call it the gunk compartment. Everybody has gunk.

I'm pretty pleased with the decision to make this call. Several things about it appeal to me, most of all its clarity. It is a binary decision. Either this will happen or that will happen. No third dish appears on the menu. The vegetarian option is off. Each alternative comes with its own assembly instructions, and helpful diagrams showing A, B and Z, and something that may be an Allen key. Or a screwdriver perhaps.

Each alternative will later come with its own consequences. I'm not interested in the consequences at this point. I couldn't care less about the consequences. I want a decision. I want to know what will happen now. Since I haven't the faintest idea what I ought to do, it was a brilliant idea to delegate the decision to an inanimate object. A telephone, in this case. Got to have confidence in the staff, and inanimate objects are a lot more reliable than human beings, in my opinion. If you want to get anywhere in life, the A303 for example, you have to know how to delegate.

If I asked you which was prettier, a cobweb or the Taj Mahal, how would you answer?

Exactly. You couldn't. You'd say it was a ridiculous question. I could delegate the question to God, and let God get on with it, but I don't really believe in God. In fact, I'm not sure I should be giving him a capital letter. I'll withdraw it at once. Words don't have capital letters when they're just thoughts, you may object: thoughts are all in lower case, like websites. That may be true of other people's thoughts. Mine do have capital letters, where appropriate, along with various other formatting.

Where was I? No, I don't believe in god, at least not today, but I do believe in Fate. I probably believe in some combination of the two. Let's call it Gate for convenience. And I like where Gate seems to be leading me. Not that I have the first idea where it is leading me. It could be anywhere. That's all right. Anywhere will do.

I think the car behind may be following me.

There may be another reason why my decision appeals to me. It's a gamble. That's fashionable these days. You can't turn on the TV without seeing adverts for gambling. I think it must be compulsory now. It's the next stage in the ascent of capitalism. First phase, the manufacturing economy. Second phase, the service economy. Third phase, the gambling economy. I expect we could all earn a decent living by cashing in each other's chips.

I have always gambled.

I've earned my living by gambling, by betting on whether the price of a commodity will rise or fall. I have traded futures. We don't call it gambling, of course, especially not now. At least, I don't imagine we do. I wouldn't know since I'm not employed in futures any more. I expect we call it, oh I don't know, predictive commodity analytics, or something. Only with capital letters. It would have to have capital letters. And initials. 'We use our own PCA model here,' I expect Rupert Loxley says to his clients, not that he probably has many clients these days. Serve him fucking right.

It's not a large step from betting on whether coffee will rise or fall to betting on whether Matthew Oxenhay will rise or fall, so I'm pretty cool about it. The only rule of gambling is a calm acceptance of whatever happens. I have dwelt in this small niche where the financial markets embrace Buddhism. Om I god.

Not only have I gambled, I've been superstitious with it too. I would trade some commodities on a Thursday, but not on a Tuesday. I would sign important deals with my left hand, even though I'm right-handed. My colleagues thought I was a genius. Perhaps best of all was that I would buy coffee futures only when it was raining. That started as a joke. One day in the '80s, it occurred to me that my last few trades in coffee had been on days when it had rained. After that I started to do it deliberately. I kept a notebook which compared my record in buying coffee with my record in buying other commodities. My record on coffee was above average.

I'm oversimplifying here. I didn't buy coffee every time it rained, or my firm would have owned the world's supply several times over. What I mean is that, when I was wondering whether it might be a good moment to buy coffee, when I was mulling it over on the Northern Line on the way to work, I let the weather that day make the decision for me.

For some reason, I got fired. What had constituted genius for forty years now constituted being a prat. Takes one to know one, as I said to Rupert Loxley. I may not have said that to him. I have called him a great many things in my head, all of them abusive, and I now get confused as to which of them I've actually said to him in person. Let's just say that he wouldn't be in the least surprised to know that I consider him a prat.

The car behind is still following me. Of course it is. It wouldn't be behind me otherwise.

Anyway, I got fired. When was that? It was on a Friday. That's when it was. A Friday about five months ago, if my memory serves me right, which it doesn't often these days.

There have been times since, I must admit, when I've thought I might be going a bit off the rails. No one else has noticed, or not much. You'd have to know me pretty well to tell anything was wrong. I've managed to keep a lid on it. But I haven't deceived myself. The fact is that I seem to have depended on the job rather more than I thought I did. So, when it wasn't there any more, it drew attention to various other failings.

The point is, and this is the important point, that it's never too late to change. That's why I'm so pleased with my decision. It will bring change. Don't ask me what sort of change. That's the type of question old farts used to ask when I was at university. 'It's all very well knocking things down, but what are you going to replace them with, blah-blah-blah?' Something better, you old fart. Change is good. Whatever comes out of this change will be good. All being well, I'll even start liking myself again. I found myself quite

6

liking myself this afternoon, as a matter of fact. That came as a surprise. It's been years since I last liked myself. Things must be getting better.

That car has turned off. It can't have been following me. Well, it was following me, because it was behind me for ten miles. But it wasn't intending to follow me. Now I come to think of it, there may be some pills in the glove compartment.

I really ought to make the call.

It's getting late and it's not far to the M3 now. What's the time? 6:35 and 30 seconds. Peep. Peep. Peep. There was a sign to somewhere back there. London, possibly.

What did I say the time was? 5:35. That's right. No, I said it was 6:35. But it's 5:35. The clocks have gone back an hour. They do that at this time of year.

When I was younger and some mates and I had spent several hours in rambling conversation, sorting out the world's miseries, sometimes we would stop and examine how we had reached that particular point. We would retrace the straight lines, the arcs and the tangents, the logic and the non sequiturs that had led from this topic to that topic, and thence to here.

Driving up this pissing awful road, I am trying to work out how this all started. How

7

I've reached the point of being about to make this call. To answer the question, there are about twenty-seven different explanations and the mix 'n' match option is available. You can take the liquorice thingies and the pear drops, but pass on the gobstoppers and the toffee crunch. There has been no one single cause. There has been a cauldron of toxic ingredients, simmering for years and suddenly coming to the boil. Like if you put sodium cyanide, strychnine and batrachotoxin into a pot, gave it a good stir and chucked in a stick of dynamite. OK, I'm showing off. I don't know what the hell I'm talking about. I was looking at Angela Jones's legs when we did Chemistry.

Where was I? Well, why don't we go back to my sixtieth birthday party.

2

When I was small, my mother showed me how to grow a carrot from a carrot. She filled a jam jar with water, cut the top off a carrot, ran a cocktail stick horizontally through the stub and suspended it over the jar, just touching the water. In time, roots sprouted, and when they were long enough and strong enough, the plant was translated to the garden and new carrots grew. This was one of the many exciting ways in which I was prepared for adult life.

It was on my sixtieth birthday, five months ago, May 2008, that I remembered this. We were having a party at home. I say 'we', but what I mean is that Judy was having a party and I was a guest, which is not surprising since I am Judy's husband and the party was being held in my honour. It was a small affair. I insisted on that when Judy proposed the idea, hoping my instruction would be ignored in favour of no party at all. I think about twenty people were there: our close friends and family. I say 'our', but what I mean is Judy's close friends and, though they are our children, what feels like Judy's family.

I wasn't remotely sober when the evening started. That was the first mistake. After forty minutes or so, I made my excuses, left the lawn and withdrew to the house. I was intending to visit the cocktail cabinet and down a large Scotch for additional fortification. Which I did. Having done so, instead of returning to the lawn, I poured a larger one and went upstairs.

I spent a few minutes in front of the bedroom mirror, taking an inventory of myself at sixty. Several things had gone missing since a previous inventory ten years earlier. Two teeth. A thousand strands of hair. Vaguely contemporary clothes. A reliable erection. There had been some gains, though. Let's not forget those. An interesting pot belly in the making. Plenty of lines going in various directions. Not of W. H. Auden proportions, but impressive. A pair of bi-focals. Summing it up, I felt that I looked spectacularly normal. Exactly what you'd expect of a well-fed Englishman at sixty. A perfect makeweight in an identity parade.

I then walked to the bedroom window and looked out over the lawn on a perfect May evening. One advantage of this perspective was that I couldn't see the house. The garden is all right, as long as you like gardens where stray leaves get court-martialled and birds can't crap without written permission. The house dates from the time between the wars when the country had temporarily mislaid its architects. It sprawls in all directions at once, like a jellyfish on a beach, devoid of structure. It has three bedrooms and the same number of utility rooms. We could never think what to do with them, so we bought things we didn't need to fill them. The only advantage of this house is that Judy likes it so much she has stopped demanding a move every five years.

The scene from the window was a distillation of life present, of life cumulative to date. I was in the house that several decades of meaningless endeavour had procured, looking down on the wife that several months of conventional courtship had procured, on the friends that the procured wife had deemed suitable for such a house and such a marriage, on the children that several episodes of drunken sex had procured, and on the partners that said children's market value had procured. None of it seemed to have a great deal to do with me. And nothing whatsoever to do with how I had imagined my life forty years earlier.

It was this that made me think of the carrots. Because what Judy had done, it seemed to me, was to cut me off in my prime, suspend me in water for a while, then transplant me to other soil, her soil, to produce a different carrot. I felt a pang of nostalgia for the original carrot that had been sacrificed to this endeavour. Thinking of that metaphor now, it seems to have lost the epic quality of a Biblical vision that it had when it occurred to me, but still to represent a truth. All I would change is to extend the accusation levelled at Judy, and include myself on the charge sheet for letting it happen. I would also indict Life, which has less capacity to wriggle out of that charge, or any other. Life is the ideal defendant when one is looking for a conviction.

What I thought most was how little all this was, how very little.

I've never envied my parents' generation. I've never envied my grandparents' generation. Nor do I envy my children's generation, nor their children's. As a matter of fact, there is no future generation that I envy, and precious few in the past.

But everybody envies us. Everybody thinks that our bums landed in the butter, that we have danced the last tango. The first third of our lives was funded by our parents and the State; the last third is supposedly being funded by our children and the State. Possibly we were self-supporting in the middle third. We are allegedly the one generation to be universally envied, and to envy no one. Except it's not true. In reality, we envy more than any of our enviers, and what we envy is our own youth and how it amounted to so little. What we mistook for the promised land turned out to be a grazing pasture en route to a land of promises. Our generation made the great mistake of peaking too soon, in fact barely after we'd arrived.

Judy had bought a new dress for this occasion, or at least I thought she had. I may have been mistaken. I don't notice her dresses. They come from the smartest boutique in Barnet, which is not saying a great deal. She dyes her hair these days, or at least I think she does. I don't like to ask, but it seems more black than it did a few years ago. She certainly has it styled at the smartest salon in Barnet, which is saying even less. In short, Judy has succeeded in turning into her mother, and I have failed to prevent myself turning into my father.

She was talking to the chief executive of my company, the long and grinding toad called Rupert Loxley. He had not fired me at this point; for him, that pleasure lay ahead. Judy was talking to him because she still believed she was living in the era in which it was thought that if a man had a charming wife it would help his career. I've tried explaining to her that I might as well be bumming a

Lithuanian rent boy for all the difference it would make, but she doesn't believe me. She was talking to him because she knew that he had got the job, three years earlier, that I had expected to get and thought I deserved to get. And because she suspected that I might not have accepted that rejection with the requisite good grace, and hoped that her charm might repair whatever harm I had done to my prospects.

Judy's children, who I'm obliged to admit are also my children, were talking to each other's partners. Whether this was an active choice, or out of indifference towards the other guests, was debatable. Sarah, our daughter, was talking to Zoë, partner of Adam, our son. Adam was talking to Rufus, Sarah's partner. I couldn't hear what they were saying. I didn't need to. Adam and Rufus would be discussing which computer games they had downloaded, and how many thousands of virtual people they could kill with them. At their age, I was going on peace demos to save the lives of real people, but what the hell.

Sarah and Zoë would be engaged in a wide-ranging conversation comprising, but by no means limited to, the noise levels in various clubbing establishments, the record amount each had spent in a day on designer clothes, the best Taylor Swift song ever, the relative merits of Tristan da Cunha and the Nicobar islands as holiday destinations, and twenty original ways of styling your pubic hair. As far as I could see, Sarah was not wearing a bra. She seldom did. It was her only known act of rebellion against her mother. I think she thought that it made her a feminist.

I could go on, but what's the point? I expect you think I'm exaggerating, that I have a jaundiced view of the young. I am not so limited in my prejudices. I have a jaundiced view of everyone, myself most of all. People a few years older than Sarah and Adam are now running the country, which is terrifying. Their idea of the long term is something that will look good in next Sunday's papers. Tony Blair apparently told Roy Jenkins that he wished he'd studied history at university. I think we all wish that, don't we?

As for the friends who were there that evening, all I can say is that they weren't. Friends, I mean, although they might as well not have been there either. They were acquaintances who now needed to be called friends because of the countless times we had seen them.

So I was spending my sixtieth birthday, supposedly the celebration of a notable achievement, looking out of my bedroom window, drinking whisky, thinking that my adult life had been pretty pathetic. At some point, rather later than I had expected, Judy must have noticed my absence and she came indoors to find me.

'There you are, Matthew. What on earth are you doing up here?' Her eyes travelled to my whisky glass, which has become their default point of focus, and she supplied her own answer. 'How many have you had?'

'I've had a few,' I said. 'But, then again, too few to mention.'

'It's not a very good idea to get tight when your boss is here.'

'Why did you invite him, then? I didn't want to see him.'

'Matthew, I think you might make an effort. Tonight of all nights. Everyone's come to see you.'

Everyone had not come to see me. Everyone would rather be sitting at home in their slippers, watching TV and eating beans on toast. Our children and their partners had come because Judy had applied a three-line whip. Everyone else had come because they had been invited six months ahead of time and were not bright enough to come up with an excuse.

'Oh I see,' I said. 'I'm so sorry — I didn't realize. Simply everyone has come to see me.

16

Le tout Barnet has come to see Matthew Oxenhay. What a popular man I must be.'

'Please, Matthew. Just tonight. For my sake.'

I sighed.

'You never used to be like this.'

'I'll be down in a few minutes,' I said.

'Please won't you come down with me now?'

'Stop hassling me, Judy. I'll be down in a few minutes.' I think I may have seen a tear in her eye as she left the room.

I felt like a shit. I knew exactly what Judy meant, that her reproaches were mild in the circumstances. I hated myself for the way I behaved at times and, the more I hated myself, the more I behaved that way. I wondered sometimes whether I was trying to make Judy hate me, trying to provoke her into leaving me. If so, that would be a poor strategy. Judy is not the leaving type. Judy is the soldier-on-and-make-the-best-of-it type. We might as well come from different generations. In fact, we do.

Judy is four years older than me, born in 1944. You wouldn't think that four years should make much of a difference, but when it is those four years, they do. She and most of her contemporaries grew up as conform-ists, and I and most of mine grew up as rebels. We wanted to change the world. They wanted to make it safe. One consequence is that Judy's lot are now content with life, and mine are bloody furious.

When we met, Judy was a secretary. Of course she was; what else would she have been? That generation of women all became secretaries. Or at least the ones that didn't become nurses or dentists' receptionists or librarians. She stopped work, paid work I mean, when she first became pregnant, never to resume it. You could say that she sacrificed her own life to create a comfortable life for me and our children. That may be true, but it is too mundane a view. Judy's life has been devoted to something more cosmic. Before marrying me, she was already betrothed to the idea of the nuclear family, to the security of the cocoon that could be woven around it. I was thought to be a suitable, if incidental, vehicle for the consummation, and for that reason I could be loved. Judy would not say that she had sacrificed her life. Judy would say that she had been fulfilled. No progressive social theorist could convince her otherwise.

You may wonder how Judy and I ever came to marry, or even got as far as a first date. I was twenty-three when we met. I had submitted to the compulsory experience of doomed romanticism. I was now surrounded by plenty of emancipated young women who thought it was cool to screw around. I'm not complaining, because I thought it was cool to screw around too, and I don't want to be thought a hypocrite. But, just as I'm sure that there were plenty of cool young women secretly hoping for a man who would not screw around, so there were plenty of cool young men hoping for a woman ditto. There was some issue of supply and demand here, but we were all into Marxist economics at the time. No one was a supply-sider then.

Judy did not screw around. In fact, it took quite some time to get her to screw at all. Funnily enough, that was a large part of her attraction. I think I always knew that we were coming from different directions. For me that was refreshing, and perhaps it was for her too. Unfortunately, we also had different destinations in mind. When you are trying hard to be attractive to someone, you minimize the differences between you. Possibly that is the worst mistake humans habitually make. It might be better to exaggerate the differences and see if the relationship survives. The differences will surface sooner or later, and by then it may be too late.

If two people stand in the same place and set out on a shared journey, and if one starts walking at an angle that is one degree different from the other, after thirty-five years, which is how long we've been married, the two of them will be miles apart. If I were a mathematician, I could tell you how many miles after thirty-five years at 4 mph, which is what Baden-Powell determined to be the proper pace for a Boy Scout. Since I was looking at Angela Jones's legs in Maths too, I can only say that it feels like thousands of miles, and very probably is.

It was another twenty minutes and two whiskies later before I came downstairs. Judy looked crestfallen. Everyone was standing around waiting for me. There seemed to be an expectation that something significant was about to happen. I was issued with a Prosecco, and Adam and Rufus wheeled a small trolley through the French windows with a large cake upon it. It was one of those bespoke cakes made at home by women who don't pay tax, for which they charge outrageous prices plus VAT, which they don't pay either.

This one was an artist's impression of the Bank of England, much as the Bank is itself these days. It had an iced inscription on the roof that read '60 YEARS OLD AND STILL KING OF THE FUTURES'. Rupert Loxley pretended to find this amusing. I lopped a large slice off the cake — the first of many slices to be lopped off the Bank this year, it now occurs to me — and everyone clapped and laughed as if it was the cleverest thing they had seen. Judy said a few words of breathtaking banality and then it was my turn.

I can't say I wasn't warned. As with any event that Judy organizes, every last element of it was predictable. I had no excuse not to be prepared to give a speech, not to have thought of a thesaurus of inanities to suit the occasion. If I had, I might have redeemed the rest of my behaviour that evening. At the very least, I might have expressed some gratitude to Judy.

But I hadn't prepared anything. I had deliberated and procrastinated before copping out with a decision to be spontaneous for once in my life. I knew it was a mistake when I decided on it; even more so when I opened my mouth. On the spur of that moment, it seemed like a funny idea. I would, briefly, recapitulate the flaws and inadequacies of everyone present. Just as people were starting to become uneasy, I would proceed to catalogue my own flaws and inadequacies. Then I would conclude that it's our failings that make us lovable, or some such crap, and aver my deepest love for all present.

It may not have been a good idea in the

first place. Combining the sincere with the insincere seldom works: it's best to stick to one or the other, in this case the latter. It is also true that I dwelt on everyone else's flaws and inadequacies for longer than I had intended. I was approaching the bit about my own flaws when I felt my legs subsiding. I slipped, with some elegance I believe, into a nearby wicker chair and passed out.

When I awoke, it was the early hours of the morning. No lights were on in the house. The patio doors were locked. It was surprisingly warm, though, and several near-empty bottles of flat Prosecco still littered the lawn, so I poured them into one bottle and sat in my wicker chair, sipping from it and pondering the nature of existence. Shortly after seven, when I had disappeared into the shrubbery at the side of the house for a pee, Sarah and Adam walked out onto the patio. I stood around the corner and eavesdropped.

'I wonder where he's got to,' said Sarah.

'Fucked off, with any luck,' said Adam.

'Don't be like that. He needs help.'

'He's not getting any from me. Not after last night.'

'He didn't mean it. You know that.'

'Saz, I'm past caring whether he means it or not. If he doesn't mean it, why does he keep doing it?'

'Because he's miserable.'

'What's he got to be miserable about?'

'Work,' said Sarah. 'That's what Mum thinks. It's why she invited his boss to the party.'

'If you ask me, things started to go wrong when he didn't get the top job,' said Adam. 'That's when the drinking started. How long ago was that?'

'About three years. Exactly the time that Mum was ill.'

'I hate to think how much booze has gone down the hatch since then. It's about time he got a grip on it.'

'It can't have been easy for him,' said Sarah. 'He was brilliant with Mum, even if he was on the bottle. All that time he took off work to look after her. It must have been a really difficult time for him.'

'Well, it was a bloody difficult time for Mum too. And she coped with it a lot better than Dad did. I don't know how she puts up with him, Saz. And I don't know *why* she puts up with him.'

'He's not himself, Adam. You can see that, can't you?'

'It's how he's been for three years. How much longer do we give him?'

Sarah sighed.

'Come on,' said Adam. 'I've got to go in a

few minutes. Let's get some coffee.'

They went back inside, and I manoeuvred my way back to the wicker chair and the remains of the Prosecco. I would like to say I felt chastened, but I didn't. There was nothing I had heard I didn't already know, or couldn't have guessed. Actually, that's not quite true. I hadn't realized Judy was sniffing into my situation at work. That would have to be watched. Otherwise, I still appeared to have one child a little on my side. The problem was that I was more inclined to agree with the other. I was beyond redemption.

Was that when it started, with Judy's illness and my being passed over? It was a difficult time, certainly. I remember a feeling of utter impotence. There was nothing I could do, except be there. At least I did that. Adam was right. That was when the drinking started. No: that was when the drinking got out of control. And Adam was also right to say that Judy was a coper. It was her illness, but she coped with it much better than I did. I nearly went to pieces. Not the best time to be under the microscope for promotion. But I don't know that it started then. I think it may have started way earlier, before Judy even. I think it may have started when I lost my brother, when I lost faith in the indissoluble goodness of life. I don't think I've ever expected things to go right since then.

Sarah must have seen me from the kitchen. A little while later, she came into the garden with two mugs of coffee and sat in the chair next to mine.

'How are you feeling, Dad?'

'Dreadful.' Neither of us said anything for several minutes. 'Come on, Saz,' I said. 'You'd better tell me. How bad was it?'

'It was pretty bad.'

'Really bad?'

'Really, really bad.'

I paused before the big question. 'How's your mother?'

'Not good. She's very upset.'

'And what about you, Saz?'

'I'm all right. You let me off quite lightly. I don't think Rufus is very amused, though. And Adam certainly isn't. Why did you pick on him like that?'

'Because he's my son.'

'So?'

'It wasn't what I intended,' I said. 'It came out wrong.' I tried to explain to her what I had meant to say, what I hadn't got round to saying before I passed out.

'Perhaps you decided to collapse when you'd said everything you really wanted to say.'

'Saz. No.'

'That was how it sounded. *In vino veritas.* Payback time.'

'For what?'

'How should I know?' Another long pause. 'Why are you so unhappy, Dad?'

'Am I?'

'Aren't you?'

'I suppose I must be, Saz. On the one hand, I'm unhappy about nothing. On the other, I'm unhappy about everything. Does that make sense?'

'No.'

'No. Perhaps it doesn't.'

'Is that why you're drinking so much?'

'I've always liked a drink.'

'Not like this.'

'Last night was exceptional,' I said. 'You've got to admit that.'

'You've been building up to it.'

'How do you know, Saz? You hardly ever see me.'

'There are telephones, Dad. Those strange devices you think live only in offices. I talk to Mum quite a lot. She's been worried about your drinking for months.'

'So that's what you do, is it? Gossip about me behind my back?'

'Would it be better if we weren't concerned for you?'

'No. I know. I'm sorry.'

'Why did you keep referring to Mum as Eva Braun?'

'Did I?'

'Yes. At least half a dozen times. It wasn't funny the first time.'

'What else did I say about her?'

'I don't think I'm going to tell you. It would make your apology even more impossible. Your best defence is drunkenness and amnesia.'

'What did I say about Rupert Loxley?'

'You said his was an extraordinary achievement. Not only promoted one rung above his level of competence, but an entire ladder.'

'I didn't say that.'

'You did.'

'Did he laugh?'

'No.'

'No, he wouldn't. He doesn't have a sense of humour.'

'It's none of my business, Dad,' she said, 'but is everything all right at work?'

No. Everything was not all right at work.

These are difficult times. The financial sector is in meltdown. It was in turmoil even in May. Futures were hard to predict. The price of some commodities was going through the roof; the price of others was tumbling. Who could say where any of them would be in a few months' time? Less business was being transacted and, since we earned our income from commissions, less income was being earned. Bonuses had been cut. At the previous board meeting, there had been a long discussion on how much routine work might be delegated to unpaid interns. Rupert Loxley had talked about the possible need to downsize; the imperative need to make the company fit for purpose. I was doodling on a piece of paper, filling in my Bingo card of clichés. No one understood when I shouted, 'House!'

We'd had similar debates over the years, at other moments of crisis, using other jargon, whatever was fashionable at the time. I used to participate with enthusiasm, but not now. Then, it would have been unthinkable that I might be one of the casualties. Now, it had become not unthinkable. It was probably being thought.

I suspected that, one morning soon, in the coming weeks or months, Rupert Loxley would ask to see me. He would not take me out to lunch: that would expend too much valuable time on a spent asset. If I were lucky, I would get a cup of coffee in his office. He would not fire me, or sack me, or even make me redundant. Those words aren't used any more. He would let me go, or say I had been selected for early retirement. Something positive; something that would make me sound

28

wildly free to have been so released, immeasur-
ably privileged to have been so selected. He
would not discuss the vulgar minutiae of money.
That would be left to the Finance Director.
Then the Inhuman Resources Director would
administer empathy and I would go home. It
would be in the morning, I was sure. A Friday
morning. Early enough for me to be forgotten
by the end of the day; early enough for it not
to spoil their weekends. I knew how these
things worked.

'Of course everything's all right, Saz. Why
shouldn't it be?'

'You're so bloody stubborn,' she said. 'How
can anybody help you when you won't let
them?'

'If I need help, I'll ask for it.'

'We won't hear you if you're dead.'

'All right,' I said. 'All right. I screwed up. I
apologize. I will perform any obeisance
required of me at the altar of decorum. I will
try not to do it again.'

It turned out that a great deal of obeisance
was required over the following days. I made
my peace with Judy, who is a kind and
understanding and forgiving woman, and a
woman who loves me, none of which facts I
may have mentioned previously. I allowed
Judy to dictate the terms of the armistice on
behalf of the other injured parties, to

29

determine the reparations that needed to be made. I had to deal with the idiot Rupert Loxley myself. I don't think my jibe about him had any bearing on what proved to be about to happen. Really not. It would have happened anyway. My only regret on that front was that I failed to say in public that he was the biggest arsehole I had ever met. But I never got to the section on his good points.

It would be easy to say that my birthday party was the beginning of the road that has led me to here, but it wasn't. That evening was itself the accumulation of months and years and decades. My speech, spectacular though it may have been, was less important in the scheme of things than my reflections standing at the bedroom window. Even so, as my history teacher used to say, for events to happen there needs to be both fertile ground and a specific seed. Angela Jones didn't take History, so I remember that. I think we can agree that the ground was highly fertile. I can hardly conceive of a greater quantity of shit. Something else was required to seed it and to spark the methane.

3

As forecast, one Friday morning, two or three weeks after the party, Rupert Loxley poked his head round my door and asked if we could have a quick word in his office.

'I'm not quite sure how to put this, Matthew,' he began.

'In that case, shall I go away until you are?'

'No. Don't do that. What I mean is, these are difficult times. Well, aren't they?' I said nothing. 'Yes, well they are. You know that. The Chairman and I have been talking. We are agreed that the company needs to be more flexible going forward. If we don't do it ourselves, it will be forced upon us, so we need to be proactive. We don't want to lay anybody off. That's the last thing we want to do. We thought — that is to say, the Chairman thought, and I think there's a lot to be said for it — that we should consider moving some of our staff on to a freelance basis, to make us lighter on our feet. We would like to offer you the position of senior consultant with the firm.'

I gave the bastard full marks for the attempt. This was a euphemism that had not occurred to me.

'What will the hourly rate be?'

'Five hundred pounds,' said Loxley. 'Very generous, I'm sure you'll agree.' He had visibly relaxed. The idiot seemed to think I was about to accept.

'And the number of hours?'

'That will be for you to determine, Matthew. The sky's the limit. Go out and get whatever you can.'

'Good,' I said. 'I think I'll start with my existing clients.'

'No, no. That's not really the point of the exercise, is it? Besides, we've asked Jason if he wouldn't mind taking over your portfolio. It would have to be new business.'

'You must think I'm as big a twat as you are,' I said.

'There's no need for that attitude. To be honest, we're making you a very generous offer. Let's face it, Matthew, things have been slipping a bit lately, haven't they? Many companies would be showing you the door right now.'

'How do I spot the difference?'

'Senior consultant. Yes or no?'

'You've got to be joking,' I said. 'Be a man for once and fire me.'

So he did. Actually, he didn't: he made me redundant, which was better. I was asked to clear my desk by the end of the morning and was offered a large severance package. Why should I have been surprised?

Life changes, and has to change. One may be becalmed for a while, but in the long run stasis is not an option. After I had been passed over for chief executive, I became a member of that most endangered of species: an ageing high earner going nowhere. I was permanently becalmed.

I had learned to read the runes; I'd too often seen them written for others. At the previous board meeting, the youngest director, recently appointed against my advice, urged the need for us to be more scientific in our approach, ridiculed the use of gut instinct in a technological age. His eyes never once met mine, but his sights were trained on me. Decades ago, when I joined the board, I had made more or less the same speech. I too never looked at the port-ridden soak at which it was aimed, whose job I envied and later got. We can fight battles only with the weapons we have. When we are young, we take up arms on the side of science, because art — in this context — requires experience, and we do not have experience. When we are older, we take up arms on the side of art, because experience is our advantage, and because we can no longer be bothered to keep pace with the science. Domestic battlefields are no different. Men bear physical arms; women emotional ones. We always choose the weapon that is most lethal in our own hands.

In my opinion, buying futures is an art, not a science. When I was the blue-eyed boy, no one questioned my methods. No one then told me not to buy futures by sniffing the air. My record was much the same as it had always been. I made mistakes. We all did. It was impossible not to in this business. All right, maybe I'd recently been making a few more than usual. I'd had an unlucky run. But I was still a match for Jason the boy scientist, the young man who wanted my job.

Why should I have been surprised? I had expected to be fired, so you'd think the actual event should not have come as a shock. But it did. It felt as much a thunderbolt as if it had fallen from a clear blue sky. I didn't go home immediately. I collected my thoughts in a bar for the rest of the day, and returned home at the usual hour. On the journey back, it struck me that my thoughts, far from being collected, were strewn all over the train carriage. I thought I would buy myself time by failing to mention to Judy what had happened.

Money was the least of my problems. I feel bad saying that, when the financial crash is finally happening and there are about to be so many people left to pick up the tab for our greed. But we were all right, and always would be. I had earned a lot of money over the years. Once the mortgage had been paid off and the children had left home, we saved most of it. Any normal person would say we had an extravagant lifestyle. But normal people don't work in the City or earn City money, and by those standards we were frugal. Then there was the redundancy money. Then there would be the company pension, which was also substantial. Then, at some point, we would decide we didn't need such a large house, so there would be a cash windfall from downsizing. No: money was the least of my problems.

When rich people say that money doesn't matter, everyone else thinks, 'Well, try living without it.' So I'm not going to say that it doesn't matter, but it isn't a cure-all. Poverty is always shit. If you can escape that, there are times when it's better to have less rather than more. This was one of them. With less money, I would have been forced to do other work, however badly paid, however different from what I was used to. I expect I would have found something, even now. With less money, I could not have sat around all day drinking and feeling sorry for myself. With less money,

I would have felt I had some purpose in life.

I spent that first weekend of unemployment reviewing my options. If I told Judy the news, there would be consequences. Not tears and tantrums; not harsh recriminations; not even sly reminders of the birthday party. That wasn't Judy's way. Instead, there would be love and sympathy and a faint trace of pained disappointment that I had let myself down, which would be another way of saying that I had let her down. Then, on Monday morning, on Tuesday morning, in fact on every bloody morning for eternity, instead of leaving home for the office, I would be sat at home with nothing to do, getting under Judy's feet and she getting under mine. And drinking. I couldn't imagine that I wouldn't be drinking.

In time, in very little time, Judy would start to ask what I was doing about getting another job. There was no prospect of another job that I might want to do, and the curse of money would prevent me from seeking one I didn't want. A life spent trading futures fitted me for nothing else. No City firm was hiring expensive men of my age. It was true that one or two people might have taken me on as a consultant. That prospect depressed. 'Those who can, do; those who can't, teach,' had been an adage of my youth. To which I now silently added, 'And those who can't teach, become consultants.' I could play golf. But you can't play golf all day every day, or I can't.

Judy would know most of this, at least I imagined she would. Everyone knew it. To admit to it, for either of us to admit to it, was to admit to the prospect of years, perhaps decades, cooped up with someone with whom one no longer has much in common, if one ever had. Once, I had faced the prospect of retirement with serenity, the sort of serenity an optimist feels when a problem is distant. I would never actually retire, I told myself. I would wind down, work fewer days in the office, develop other interests. One day it would emerge that I had worked my final day and I would barely notice, so absorbing would those other interests have become. I didn't trouble to define the other interests. Now, when they were instantly required, I couldn't think what they might be. Until they materialized, there was no substitute for the working week, for my own particular working week.

So I decided to go on doing what I'd always done.

I would rise at the usual hour, shave and shower and have breakfast, put on a suit and tie and leave for work at eight a.m. It was possible that Judy would discover one day; probable that she would not. No member of my firm lived near us, nor did we see any of them socially. If Judy and I needed to communicate during the day, it was by mobile phone, and I still had mine. I ran the family finances, dealt with the bank statements, so she wouldn't know that a salary was no longer appearing on them. That left the question of how I would fill the hours between leaving and coming home.

I decided to initiate the practice of standing at the doorway of my former office and saying 'good morning' to my former colleagues as they arrived for work. In the evening, I would return and say 'good night' to them as they left. In between, I spent the day in Costa's and resisted the bars. I couldn't arrive home drunk every night.

This was satisfying so far as it went. My erstwhile colleagues had no idea how to deal with a ghost. They started by smiling at me, one or two even returning my greeting. Then they began to hurry past me, looking the other way. I enjoyed their discomfiture, but the routine soon became boring, and it hardly amounted to a long-term career.

One day, a week or two after Sack Friday, Rupert came out of the building promptly at six p.m. and looked around for me. I was surprised to see him. After the first day, he had taken to using the goods entrance to avoid me.

'Good night, Rupert,' I said.

'Good evening, Matthew. Let's go and have a drink.'

'Why?'

'I'll tell you in a minute. Let's go and have a drink.'

We installed ourselves in a nearby bar and I thought I would treat myself to a double whisky at the company's expense. Rupert drank mineral water.

'It's a long time since we've done this,' he said. I said nothing. 'In fact, not since I took over the top job.'

He looked at me challengingly. I still said nothing.

'Before that, we did it quite often. In fact we used to get on pretty well. Didn't we?'

I didn't reply. What he said was true, but I couldn't admit it.

'Matthew, I'm very sorry I got the job that you wanted. I'm also sorry that it happened when your wife was ill. But I had just as much right to want the job as you did. I didn't do you down in any way. It was a fair fight and I won it. Why do you find that so hard to accept?'

'I deserved it.'

'And so did I. We both deserved it. Only one of us could get it. At any other time in the previous ten years, it would probably have been you. The moment of decision came at the wrong time for you. I'm sorry, but that wasn't my fault. Ever since then, you've resented me. You've let yourself go. You drink too much. Your judgement has slipped. You've created a bad atmosphere in the office. You've made yourself awkward at board meetings. Other people were asking for months why I hadn't fired you.'

'What other people?'

'Almost all your senior colleagues, if you want to know. It's not that they don't like you. They're very fond of you, most of them, but they're fond of the man you were, not of the man you are. As am I, frankly. It couldn't go on. Someone had to go. Probably several people will have to go in the end. What was I expected to do? Fire someone who was doing a decent job and keep you? I tried to give you a dignified way out, but you were too bloody proud to take it. Now we have to endure your pantomime twice a day.

'Matthew, you can't go on like this. We can put up with it, if we must. You can't. It's dragging you down. It must be dragging you down. People are concerned about you, believe it or not. Now for God's sake talk to me and let's see if we can find a way out of this for you.'

'I could always top myself, if that's what you'd like.'

'Don't be ridiculous, Matthew. That's not what anyone wants.'

'What do you suggest, then?'

'Well, I do have one idea. We haven't replaced you and we're not going to. We need fewer staff, not more. So your office is still empty. If you like, and on certain conditions, I would be prepared to let you use it when you want. I can see what's happened has been a blow to you. Suddenly stopping work isn't easy for anyone. I don't know what you plan to do next, and you plainly don't either. If it would help to smooth the transition into the future, you can keep your office for a bit.'

'What are the conditions?'

'You have no role within the company. You're not on the payroll. You will not talk to any of the clients. You will not be drunk in the office, or keep drink there. You will be polite and friendly to your former colleagues. And if there is any lapse, one single lapse, in any of this, you will be out on your arse in two seconds.'

I couldn't think what to reply. I couldn't bring myself to thank Rupert, although he had in fact thrown me a lifeline. I couldn't imagine how I would stick to the terms of my parole. But I wasn't much keen on the alternative either.

Rupert stood up. 'Think about it, Matthew.

I'll come in by the front door tomorrow, and either you come up with me, or you don't. That's it. Final offer, and God knows how I've been persuaded to make it at all.'

I may have given the impression that I do not have a high opinion of Rupert Loxley, and you may have concluded that this is a product of jealousy. It would be fairer to say that it is not only a product of jealousy. Rupert is one of the diminishing breed of upper-class smoothies who once used to run every institution in the City. His upper lip was permed at birth. His type has been replaced mainly by the barrow boys who, after Big Bang, moved half a mile west from Petticoat Lane to the City. They couldn't be more different but, funnily enough, there's not much to choose between them. Belonging to neither category, I can be impartial in such judgements.

The hegemony of Rupert's breed was secured by their address books. They had long lunches during which they passed confidential information to influential friends. When the barrow boys started doing much the same thing, rather less subtly, for more overt personal gain, Rupert's breed labelled it 'insider dealing' and tried to have it outlawed. It didn't seem to dawn on them that they'd been doing the same thing themselves for generations. Their version was called having lunch with a friend, which was of course quite different. So they were hoist by their own petard, as regulators attempted to shoehorn the jungle into a municipal garden, and cocked it up completely, as is now apparent to everyone.

Ruperts are not now much to be found at the cutting edge of City life. They still vegetate in the backwaters, however, and our firm is unfortunately a backwater. The reason Rupert should not have become chief executive is because he's too soft. This is not a time for softies in the City. The bastards arrived to claim their inheritance a while ago.

Why did I ever come to work in the City in the first place? Why did they ever let me in? It beats me. I think I've been taking the piss ever since. When I talk about buying coffee futures when it's raining, that's taking the piss, isn't it? That is saying this whole system is bollocks, so let's treat it as bollocks. The other things I've done too. Maybe I haven't really done any of them, because how could I have been so successful if I had? Maybe I tell myself I have, to make me sound less like one of them. Maybe I've done it the same way as the rest of them, only better. Perhaps the truth of the matter is that the one thing in life for which I seem to have any aptitude is something for which I have the utmost contempt.

No decent chief executive would have made that offer. You don't need to be a genius to see that if everyone who loses their job is allowed to go on sitting in their offices rent free, there will be a problem. I was not the only one likely to lose his job in this company. If the moron Rupert Loxley allowed me to stay, he would be setting a precedent. This would do nothing to bolster his already limited authority. Even without lifting a finger to encourage it, I would become a magnet for any discontent in the company.

Rupert was soft to offer me the option, and I would be soft if I took it. Did I have no pride left? Strangely enough, no; I didn't. If the choice was between doing nothing in an office that wasn't mine, becoming an object of ridicule to people who had once respected me, and sitting at home with Judy getting drunk, the first option seemed preferable. I started to think about other options. And I could think of only one.

People don't expect couples to split up in their sixties. They're meant to have calmed the itches by then. Yet it strikes me as a logical time to split. There's no need for it earlier, unless you really hate each other, or have fallen in love with someone else. It had never crossed my mind to leave Judy until now. For years, she was busy with the kids and I was busy with my work. When the kids had left home, I was still busy with my work. I might have bemoaned our dreary social life. I might have wished we could have had an interesting conversation sometimes. I may have been irritated by Judy's small-c conservatism. Her big-C Conservatism too. But this was easy enough to put up with. While I was working.

It was the thought of putting up with it constantly, all day every day, for decades maybe, that was frightening. When I was small and I thought about death, it was the for ever part of it I could not comprehend. Death meant nothingness. For ever. For ever and ever. For ever and ever and ever and ever and ever and ever and ever. That was how the rest of my life with Judy now felt: nothingness stretching to infinity. It wouldn't be to infinity, of course, because at some point I'd die. Then it would be back to the other for ever. I found it hard to distinguish between the two.

But the alternative was no better. A divorce would be expensive. Those sandbags of money stacked against the floodwaters would be halved. Any judge would take a generous view of Judy's contribution to our assets, and be right to do so. The water would probably still not seep in, but who could say that for certain at the moment? Anyway, that was not the issue. Taking risks with money came as second nature to me. Nor, to be honest, were those future years to be spent with Judy the entire issue. The issue was the future years to be spent with myself. Whether Judy was there to share them was almost beside the point. The point was the nothingness. My nothingness.

Judy's preferred course through life, dead and dated though it was, fitted her better for circumstances, for any circumstances, than mine did. She had few expectations, and no illusions. Judy had spent a lifetime adapting, a lifetime keeping house, a lifetime making small talk in local shops, a lifetime transporting plants around the garden, a lifetime seeding and cultivating friendships, a lifetime making herself available for the children. Those skills would never go to waste. They would always be in fashion. How they had managed to satisfy a day, let alone an eternity, was beyond me. But they had. I had no such hinterland to fall back upon.

I was standing on the pavement outside the office door when Rupert Loxley arrived the next morning, and we went upstairs together.

4

I thought I would walk that afternoon. The clouds hung low in the sky, burdened by a weight of rain, but it was not falling. It was one of those English late-summer days that feel like March. From my office off Leadenhall Street, through the thoroughfares of the City, towards St Paul's, I stepped on pavements damp only from the promise of rain. As a teenager, I had walked these dead-beat streets on feet of clay. They were coloured grey then, and they were coloured grey now. Nothing changes much.

Idling over the Millennium Bridge, early for my appointment, not early enough to take time for a coffee, I paused midstream and looked to the east. The Thames coruscated beneath, sequinned water shimmering in the current. The tide was out. Plastic bottles, pickled wood, an old shoe, two gnawed sheets of polystyrene littered the mud on the foreshore. In the distance, Canary Wharf was truncated by cloud. There was no refuge from the monochrome; it watermarked the city. Grey pushing down from above; grey pushing up from below; the world compressed into reluctant contemplation of itself. No birds. I don't think there were any birds.

Days like these inspired me. Others found them dismal, but I loved them. London was nearly mine again when it was like this, when I was able to soft-shuffle down its streets on pavements where each succeeding footstep faded away. When I was young, I used to think of myself as a plane tree, growing new bark to clothe me, shedding old bark to keep me naked. I was invisible in the city's throng, my thoughts my own, omnipotent and anonymous. No one knew the dreams I harboured. London was mine.

It may have been a drab affair, that old London, the London of the post-war years, but in the drabness lay its soul. The city seemed anaesthetized by the past, weighed down by its history, its recent history anyhow. Everywhere lay reminders of the war. Craters pockmarked the city, filled with rainwater and the remnants of homes. Squares were delineated by the stumps of railings melted down for tanks and artillery. Buddleia and foxgloves tenanted the wastelands. There was no fevered effort to rebuild what had been destroyed, not yet. Tower blocks had yet to scar the landscape. Dilapidated hoardings patrolled the bombsites, slats missing, front doors for feral cats and errant children.

This was the world I sprang from. That London had been stolen now. I no longer owned it, and I didn't much care for the new proprietors. Just before I left school, they showed the sixth form films on possible career choices. The one on the City was called 'My Word is my Bond' and no one laughed when it was screened.

I had a meeting at Tate Modern. I would find an executive from our PR company at the main entrance, and we were to see the director. He was trying to sell us on becoming corporate sponsors and our PR company thought this a good idea. These days, PR people think any idea a good one if it appears to associate a financial institution with humanity. We are trying to accustom ourselves to this concept. We grew up thinking that only profits should accrue. With the current reputation of profits, self-certified humanity has become the preferred alternative.

It was three months since my conversation with Rupert Loxley. My presence in the office no longer caused surprise, even to me. Early June now seemed like a surreal blip in my seemingly seamless career. I had enjoyed my job, but large parts of every job are tedious, so it was rather satisfying to sit with my feet on the desk, reading the newspaper, with no need to do anything. A few times during the summer I had taken myself off to Lord's or the Oval for a day's cricket. It couldn't last for ever, of course. It was a fool's paradise, but I was a fool and this was, if not paradise, then the next best thing on offer.

I kept to the terms of my parole, for the most part, although some of the bottles of mineral water on my table might have contained vodka. I believed Rupert's threat and had no intention of triggering it. Sometimes former colleagues would drop in for a chat over coffee, and sometimes they would try to engage me in a discussion on the merits and, more especially, the demerits of Rupert Loxley as a boss. I never rose to the bait. I wouldn't have put it past him to despatch a few fifth-columnists to my office. As a result, he began to trust me. He asked if I would be interested in taking on a few light duties, and I said yes. The deal was the same: no pay. But my unpaid job started to take on a life of its own.

When, at what had turned out to be my last board meeting, we had discussed a role in the company for unpaid interns, it hadn't occurred to me that I would become one of them. There were a number of minor jobs that needed doing and which everyone else was too busy to do. This meeting was a case in point. It may sound grand, but I was there to listen and to report back, not to make decisions. Still, they couldn't have sent a twenty-year-old intern to meet the director of Tate Modern, so I was saving someone expensive an unproductive afternoon.

I knew nothing about art. Neither did anyone else in the company. We have large abstract pieces of something or other, by someone or other, decorating the white walls of our offices, which our finance director has deemed a sound investment. I used to keep a copy of a Turner on my wall, *Rain, Steam, and Speed*. It was probably one of the idiosyncrasies that made me suspect as a corporate man. It now appeared to qualify me as a connoisseur. I told Rupert I was happy to attend the meeting as long as the PR woman did the talking, as she would have done without such stipulation.

The director was Spanish, I think. I felt sorry for him. It's hard to maintain integrity with a begging bowl in one's hand. He had been well briefed, was courteous without being obsequious, and spoke to me as if to a foreigner, in more than the obvious sense. He was not the one to conclude a deal, any more than I was. The pimps in his finance department would do that. His job was to spread his legs and show us what was on offer. I seem to remember a time when not all of us were tarts. It's what comes of not making things, of only buying and selling them. Very hard to distinguish that from selling oneself, and most of us no longer try.

It came down to money, as it always does. This amount would buy a listing in the small print; that amount a lasting testament. All amounts would in the end depend for their value on the threads of news spun round them by the PR company. We talked as though such sordid considerations did not apply. Our generosity and our aesthetic sensibility were the sole agenda items, and the director and the PR woman had a mutual interest in conflating them. In due course, a proposal would come to a board meeting, along with a proposal to sponsor a wind-turbine project in Dorset, which I'd also been asked to evaluate. And the directors would debate whether our humanity was best advertised by investing in art, or by investing in wind, and whether they could tell the difference.

When the meeting ended, the PR woman needed to rush away. The director murmured polite goodbyes and departed. There was little point in my returning to the office, and I had no great desire to go home. Other, more salacious, options had once filled tight holes in tight timetables. They had lost their appeal as middle age advanced. So I was left, at the director's invitation, to roam the gallery.

When I saw her, I cannot say that I recognized her immediately. She was standing quite still, head tilted one way, then the other, hair up, a pair of rimless glasses perched on her nose, regarding what seemed to be a painting of two wind turbines on the seashore. She stepped backwards, knocked into me, turned to apologize. Something about her seemed familiar, only faintly, nothing more.

'I'm so sorry.'

'My fault for standing so close,' I said.

'I wanted to see from a distance. I should have looked.'

'What are they?' I asked. 'Wind turbines?'

'I don't think so. It was painted in 1936.'

'Oh.'

She wandered off to another part of the gallery. I stayed to look at the wind turbines. The painting was called *The Promise*, and the caption advised me that the title referred to the coming dawn, heralding possibilities of birth and growth.

I ambled round for a while longer, impersonating the art lover I might have been. Then it occurred to me that wine might be available in the café. Standing at the plate-glass window, an indifferent Beaujolais in hand, I was watching the reflections of the visitors superimposed on the sullen London skyline, when I saw her again. She was sitting at a table, on her own, stirring a cup of coffee. I walked up to her.

'Hello again,' I said.

'Hello. Are you following me or am I following you?'

'Neither, as far as I know. Do you mind if I join you?'

'Please do,' she said.

I sat on the plastic chair facing her and put my wine on the table.

'I feel a little guilty watching you drink coffee. Do you fancy some wine?'

'No thanks. It's a little early for me.'

'My body clock is set to European time,' I said. 'At least, it is at this time of day. At other times, it's set to New York or Tokyo.'

'How cosmopolitan you must be.' She was smiling.

'Not really,' I said. 'My name's Matthew, by the way.'

She took off her glasses, removed the clip holding her hair, so that it fell straight and true over her shoulders.

'Anna.'

That was when everything came back. Not everything. Not what might have been. I do not know how you recall an absence, what never was. And not what was, either, because that had never been absent, the little and everything that it was. What came back were remembrances of things beginning, of buds about to blossom, of stems snapped off, to be stored unbloomed in clouded jars.

The long fair hair was still long, and still more fair than grey. Make-up, which had been superfluous to her teenage face, was applied as sparingly as God spares his mercy. The blue-grey eyes, half fixed on me, half elsewhere, half humorous, half melancholic, were unchanged in their contradictions.

She wore faded blue jeans, tucked into long brown leather boots, and a loose-knit, loosely worn jersey in harlequin colours that on another woman would have obscured a perfect figure. On her it accentuated it.

There is never the measure of time we believe there to be. We fail to do things, confident there will be time later, to find the moment gone. We do things impetuously, fearing the opportunity will be lost, to find the moment for them not yet arrived. We are considered in our actions, and wish we had been spontaneous. We are instinctive, and regret our instincts. Never exactly the perceived measure of time; seldom the required response.

I had a choice. Anna seemed not to remember me. Or she did, and was concealing the fact. Either I could remind her that we had met before, forty-one years earlier. Or I could treat today on her terms, as an encounter with a stranger. I chose the latter.

'I don't think I understand very much of this stuff,' I said.

'You don't need to. Feel what it's saying to you.'

'It hasn't been speaking today.'

'Perhaps you don't know how to listen,' she said.

'Perhaps it has nothing to say.'

'What are you doing here? Killing time?'

'I had a meeting.'

'With?'

'With the director,' I said.

'What about?'

'What every meeting is about. Money. We were discussing corporate sponsorship.'

'You must be a banker.'

'Certainly not.'

'Something close to it.'

'I trade futures.'

'I could have done with you once,' said Anna.

And I could have done with you once, I thought. But you didn't want me and I never knew why. I said nothing. We looked at each other.

'I suppose,' she said, 'that you're one of those men who hang around art galleries, looking cultured and hoping to pick up strange women.'

'Are you a strange woman?'

'About as strange as you, I should think,' said Anna.

That was another chance untaken. I could have told her she was not a stranger; that, in July 1967, we had spent a summer afternoon together, lying in a field on Blackdown Hill in Surrey. I could have reminded her that, at the end of the afternoon, she had invited me to go to France with her.

But once I hadn't admitted to knowing her upon the first recognition, by default I had decided in favour of artifice. If I told her now, or later, or never, it would still be artifice. Nothing could undo the first concealment. And having made that decision, if you can call it a decision, I was beginning to enjoy the thrill of the deception.

For, with Anna, to start a game on level terms was to lose it. She enticed you a long way, further than you had dared hope, and at exhilarating speed. I had discovered that in '67. Yet if you were in a court of law, little in the transcript of your conversation with her would convince the jury of such an assertion. The justification lay in the difference between the words spoken and the same words written down. It was founded on inadmissible evidence. It was unarguable. To start with a cheat's advantage might change the odds.

57

It could be that I would lose this game again. It could be that if Anna had wanted me to win, she would have let me win the first time we played, that there were men with whom she did not play this game, or with whom she threw it. I didn't think so. My considered opinion, forty years in the cask, was that Anna played this game with every man, and only one smart enough to beat her at it would win her. I wondered whether she had been any-one's prize for long.

It was quite absurd of me to think like this. I barely knew her. I had barely known her at the time, and that was half a lifetime ago. I had felt then as if I knew her, as if I had known her since long before I met her. Which was the reason, one of the reasons, why the pain of losing her was so great, why I had spent hundreds more hours thinking about Anna than I'd ever spent being with Anna. All those hours thinking about her had made me believe that I knew her. Perhaps the truth was that I didn't know her at all. Perhaps that was why I had lost her.

I tried to make myself forget these precon-ceptions. I told myself that Anna would have changed, as I must have changed, that we were not the same two people. I tried to ignore the fact that it was Anna, to persuade myself I would have behaved the same way that day had she been a stranger, as I well might. In other words, I tried to take the past out of Anna. I couldn't do it. Anna had once seemed my entire future and, in failing to become that, she had become my entire past. Now here she was again.

'I do hope you're not as strange as me,' I said. 'For your sake.'

'What is strange?' She smiled and looked at her watch.

'I'm sorry. Am I boring you?'

'Not yet,' said Anna. 'I have a train to catch at some point.'

'When is it?'

'Not for a little while.'

'I don't know about you,' I said, 'but this place reminds me of a staff canteen. Would you like to go for a drink somewhere else, if there's time before your train?'

'Yes, all right. Why not?'

'What's your station?'

'Paddington.'

'We could walk across the river. I know a bar near the Mansion House. How about that?'

'If we're having a drink, a bar seems an inspired choice.'

We walked across the Millennium Bridge, a light rain now falling. Mine was the only umbrella, shielding the two of us, close together, locked in step. I did most of the talking, busking an improvised solo about London, how it had changed, how it was better but I liked it less and no longer loved it, and did that make any sense, and Anna thought it did make sense. In the bar, divested of her coat, ruffling the harlequin sweater to distress her appearance, she sipped slowly on a white wine and moved imperceptibly away from me each time I moved imperceptibly closer to her. Just as she had in 1967.

'Where does the train from Paddington take you?' I asked.

'It could take me to many places. Almost as far as my imagination. On this occasion, I hope it'll take me to Somerset.'

'Is that where you live?'

'Yes.'

'On your own?'

'That's quite an impertinent question after barely an hour, wouldn't you say?' But she was smiling. She didn't really think it impertinent. 'Anyone would think you were a teenager.'

'I thought all men were meant to be teenagers.'

'I always hope for an exception,' said Anna. 'In some respects I live alone and in others I don't. If that answers your question.' She smiled again. 'And what about you? Or is it not my place to ask questions?'

'Ask away.'

'Are you married?'

'Bloody cheek,' I said.

'I like to know where I stand.'

'So do I.'

'I think I'll take that as a yes. You look married. So this is an illicit assignation. At least, I imagine it is. Or perhaps you'll go home to your wife in . . . in Buckinghamshire, I think . . . north of London anyway — '

'Barnet.'

'Oh dear. Not your choice, I hope. Well, perhaps you'll go home to your wife in Barnet and tell her you picked up this woman at Tate Modern and took her for a drink and propositioned her.'

'I haven't propositioned you.'

'No, but you will.'

'You should be so lucky.'

I got a throaty laugh, a laugh that said that gender politics could be the funniest thing on earth, as long as I never forgot that they were also serious.

'Do you disapprove?' I asked.

'Naturally. I'm a prude. Down in Somerset we all disapprove of extramarital affairs, unless sheep are involved.'

'Sheep could be involved, if you wanted. Only as spectators, though.'

She snorted. 'We have sheep on the farm

where I live. Every year, a bloody great ram appears for a few days to service the ewes, with a pad strapped to his chest. When all the ewes have ink marks on their backs, he goes to another farm. What a great life. Unless you're a ewe, of course, and then it's only once a year. Mind you, I'd settle for that these days. I sometimes think that men should be fitted with ink pads, each with his own serial number, so we can look at our boobs and remember where we've been.'

'Whose numbers would you like on yours?'

'Jagger. Connery. Cohen.'

'Men who will slip away in the morning,' I said. Anna smiled. 'I expected someone more permanent. And more original.'

'Yes; so did I once,' said Anna. 'Whose imprint would be on your ink pad?'

'Yours.'

For a moment, Anna was taken aback. I had scored a hit. 'When I said you'd proposition me, I didn't expect it to be quite so soon.'

'That wasn't a proposition. It was a statement. An answer to your question.'

'I'll be careful about asking any more questions,' said Anna.

I don't know whether to be depressed that we don't change, or to be reassured. It depends what premium one places on consistency, I suppose. Nothing seemed to have changed between the two of us, nothing since that afternoon on Blackdown. At the time, I had hoped that the conversation we had started then would continue through our lives. To listen to us now, you would think it had, running through the years like an underground stream, now breaching the surface again. Actuarially, there had been a break of decades. Actually, there had been no break. We were dwelling in a continuum, picking up the fabric and the texture of an old conversation, humming old tunes.

When I thought of all that had happened to me in the years between, all the tangible changes to my life, all the consequent implications for my psychology, my behaviour, that one would assume, all the commensurate changes there must have been in Anna's life, it was disarming to discover that the two of us could be nineteen all over again. A little more cynical, a little more knowing, a little less naive, and yet still the same two teenagers. I didn't know whether this reflected how we truly were, or whether each of us, unconsciously, instinctively, was reaching back to the person we had once been, parodying our younger selves, trying to convince ourselves they still existed.

How many people do we meet in our lives with whom we feel in complete harmony? I struggle to think of more than a few. Anna had been one of them. How unforgivable to have squandered that opportunity.

I was not sure what to say next. This could be written off as a chance encounter, an event insusceptible to meaning, the random reappearance of an old face; its random disappearance. Or I could choose to give it meaning, to substantiate the coincidence and, Anna permitting, to translate the accidental moment into a conscious act of purpose. And, if I did that, to what end? The resurrection of a young man's dream, or the calculation of an older man's future?

When I was a child, I sat in scripture lessons and wrestled with the competing claims of predestination and free will to be the reflection of God's purpose. Now I am sceptical as to God's existence and mostly dissent from any notion of purpose. But I remain unable to escape the question and want to give the answer I wanted to give as a child, which was 'both'. The possibility that I do not have free will is intolerable. It would negate every decision I've yet made and render future ones redundant. It would extract the sole remaining point from a pointless life.

And yet. At isolated moments, few in number, rich in import, I leave my ego in the wings and summon destiny to the stage. It is not, it cannot be, a coincidence that Anna has come back into my life in this way and at this moment. There has to be a meaning, and it is demanded that I interpret the meaning and act upon it.

That is what I thought in 1967. It's what I thought sitting in The Fine Line bar with Anna. It's what I'm thinking now, driving up the A303. No matter that I appeared to have been mistaken earlier. I was not mistaken. Destiny is a notoriously poor timekeeper. It had arrived early then, now at its appointed hour.

I remembered that in July '67, the week before I met Anna, I had seen a play in the West End with Ian McKellen and Judi Dench. It was called *The Promise*. That had seemed significant at the time. Now, forty-one years later, I had met Anna again. This time, it was a painting, not a play, but it was still called *The Promise*. What more of a sign could I want?

The confidence dissipated, as it does. The insistent whisper returned: that this moment had only the meaning that we each chose to give it, of our own free will.

Anna had gone to the loo. I took the opportunity to phone Judy, explaining that the Tate meeting had gone on longer than expected and might continue for a while yet. It was impossible to know whether she believed me. I didn't really care. I had chosen the meaning I wanted to give this moment.

Anna returned. She sat down without looking at me. She rumpled her hair, then her jersey, then her hair again. I poured us each another glass of Chablis.

'What am I doing here?' she demanded. The question did not seem to be addressed to me, so I ignored it. 'What the hell am I doing here? Jesus Christ.'

A long pause followed. I raised my glass.

'Cheers,' I said.

Anna recomposed herself. 'Cheers. Here's to perfect strangers.'

'Thank you.'

'Perfect qualifies the strangeness, not you. I'm sorry. I'm not used to doing something like this.'

'Were you once?'

'Too much so,' said Anna. 'But we're not going to talk about that.'

'What are you used to now?'

'I'm used to digging my garden and pulling up vegetables. I'm used to feeding the chickens and collecting eggs. I'm used to standing at a market stall on Saturday mornings and selling my produce. I'm used to listening to Radio 4 and shouting at the politicians.'

In 1967, we had talked about what we would be doing in fifty years' time. 'I will be living,' Anna had said, 'in a small rented cottage in Dorset, drawing my pension, digging my vegetable patch, keeping chickens, and writing to the newspapers about the decline of the modern novel.' She was one county out and had yet to mention the modern novel. I had threatened to visit her in Dorset fifty years later, and to suggest we had an affair before the onset of senility. Anna had replied that she might say yes. I had asked if I would have to wait that long. 'At least,' Anna had said. At the time, I had thought we were both joking.

'Sounds idyllic,' I said.

Another laugh, a laugh that suggested Anna's life was not altogether idyllic. She translated this as: 'It's all right, I suppose.'

'Better than working, anyway.'

'You don't call that work?'

I wasn't doing well. 'Better than sitting in an office.'

'If you say so.'

I waited for another laugh, or a smile. It didn't come. I was about to say: 'This isn't like you, Anna. What's the matter? Where's the laughter?' then realized that I couldn't. I also realized it was an absurd statement. I knew nothing about her, other than how she had been one Saturday afternoon forty-one years earlier. That image had been preserved

67

in formaldehyde, a sliver of her placed in a Petri dish and used as a stem cell from which to build a complete Anna in my mind. In the process, some of the complexities had been lost, even though I knew they had been there.

'At least it sounds like freedom,' I said.

'Freedom isn't a word I use much these days,' said Anna. 'The only times in my life I've felt free are when I've been in love. It's funny. When I was a teenager, I couldn't see any connection between love and freedom. I don't think I'd ever been in love, or been loved. Freedom was a word I used all the time, then. It was a political word. I didn't think of it in the context of love. Freedom was what I wanted for the world. And for myself, of course. Freedom was what life was about. I'm quite precise with words, I think. They matter to me. They've always mattered. I'm not sure I ever paused to consider what the word freedom meant. It seemed self-evident, so I chucked it around with abandon, like everyone else, and only recently have I thought to question its meaning. Now, freedom is a word I seldom use. And, no, I don't think I'm free, except in a narrow and specific way, certainly not in any universal sense. Who is? Are you, Matthew, do you think? Are you free?'

'Not really.'

'Why not?'

'It's hard to say. I don't feel free. Everything in life is a constraint in one way or another. I never seem able to be myself.'

'And how would you be if you were yourself?'

'I wouldn't be anything in particular. I would just be.'

'I've tried that,' said Anna.

'And?'

'It's good. Up to a point.'

'Where is the point?'

'The point of loneliness,' said Anna.

'Are you lonely?'

Now Anna did laugh, and it was a relief. 'What have you got me talking about? Sneaking me into a conversation like this!'

'You started it.'

'Did I? Yes, I probably did. I get bored with small talk, don't you?'

'Constantly,' I said. 'Bored with small talk, bored with small people, bored with a small life. How often do you come to London?'

'Once or twice a year. That's enough. I stay with an old university friend in Crouch End for a few days and binge on galleries and theatre. I need the fix. Any more often and I'd start getting broody like my hens.'

'Why?'

'I'm not really a country woman. I've made

myself into one, but I'm not. I miss the buzzy metro life. If I wasn't careful, I'd find myself moving back.'

'What would be wrong with that?'

'Drugs aren't good for you,' said Anna. 'Unfortunately.'

'Would that be the voice of experience talking?'

Anna smiled. 'Haven't we reached the end of the interview yet? Is there still more you want to pump out of me?'

'I had hoped we were having a conversation.'

'A rather one-sided conversation. Still, it's better than sitting with a man who never stops droning on about himself.'

'I can do that too.'

'Well, why don't you? I've just about got time. Unless you've had an especially eventful and fascinating life, that is.' Anna delayed the smile for at least five seconds, savouring the uncertain look on my face.

I was used to making a précis of my life, to cutting and pasting sequences together for the edited highlights. There were different versions of the show. The version I used in the City, talking to clients or business acquaintances, or for an occasional job interview long ago, when greener pastures had beckoned, only to prove parched, or on offer to other grazers. The version I used at the golf club, tenuously related to the truth, a monument of braggadocio posing as self-effacement. The version I used at dinner parties, even further removed from the truth, emphasizing a jovial, uxorious man I barely recognized.

The version I needed to present to Anna should have had time for composed consideration. Neither time nor composure was available. Had the self-portrait been unvarnished, it would have revealed a study of tedium, regret and anxiety. With too much varnish, credibility and substance would have been effaced, not to mention the truth.

I did not yet know what I wanted from Anna. That's not true. I did know what I wanted. I didn't know if I was wise to seek it. I am not entirely an idiot. I've seen enough men of my age make fools of themselves as they have grown older. Usually a younger woman is involved and, in a way, a younger woman was involved now, as was a younger man. The problem was that wisdom, except to the wise, is a quality evident only in retrospect. My one decision so far was that I wanted to see Anna again. I didn't intend to say goodbye to her at a tube station and wave her out of my life for a second time. I believed that our conversation that evening had been sufficiently encouraging for her not to want it either.

Beyond that next meeting, I had no expectation as to what might happen, no opinion as to what might then seem wise or unwise. At least, I don't think I had. Now, driving up the A303, having decided what I have decided, resolved to splurge the rest of my life on a lottery ticket, I cannot trust my memory as to what I was thinking six weeks ago.

I do remember wondering whether it was possible to have Anna for a friend, to deny our carnal desires, mine anyway, and to manufacture a platonic bubble in which we could coexist from time to time. That could not be in Somerset, or not often: too many, too convoluted, excuses for Judy. Nor in London, not on any permanent basis. Anna was not the sort of woman you could install in a flat in Maida Vale and expect to be happy there. Or to be there at all.

We could meet in London, though. I could suggest that she came up more often, perhaps once a month. I could pay her fare, if she would let me. I wasn't sure she would let me: Anna seemed to prize her independence more than anything, perhaps more than she prized herself. If any of this were to happen, I would need to tell her that we had met before. And if it disconcerted her that I had not previously mentioned the fact, I could say it disconcerted me that she had forgotten me so easily. Or I could claim it was a game, that I had been waiting to see how long it would take her to remember, that no form of deception had been involved, that I had been teasing.

For now, the need was to say enough about myself to make me seem worth seeing again, and no more. Over the dregs of the Chablis, I tried to do that. I didn't mention that I was unemployed. Technically, I now wasn't. I was unpaid, which is different. Ask an intern.

'Your wife seems to have a somewhat hazy role,' said Anna.

I had played down Judy's part in my life. What else was I supposed to do in the circumstances? However, it was also true that Judy did have a hazy role in my life, as I probably had in hers.

'Doesn't that usually happen,' I said, 'when you've been married for years?'

'Usually. It's what puts me off marriage.'

'It's what puts you off permanence.'

'Nothing's permanent,' said Anna. 'No point in pretending it is. When something reaches its use-by date, you eat it or chuck it. You don't let it moulder.'

'Which will you be doing with me?'

'I don't know,' said Anna. 'You haven't reached your use-by date yet.'

'Do I take that as a compliment?'

'Not necessarily. I haven't even bought the packet.'

'What does it take to get a compliment from you?'

Anna smiled. 'Someone who doesn't fish for them. And now, Matthew, if you'll excuse me, I really must be going.'

'Can I see you again?'

'Possibly. If you're prepared to wait six months.'

'I'll be in Somerset in a few weeks' time.'

'You'll be in Somerset, or you'll be making a special journey there in the hope of seeing me?'

'I'll be in Somerset. Dorset in fact, but I expect I'll have to drive through Somerset.'

'Your satnav will probably have other ideas,' said Anna.

'They're next door to each other, aren't they?'

'Russia's next door to Canada.'

'You're trying to put me off.'

'No. Just trying to help with your scheduling. What are you doing in Dorset? Do you have another woman there? From the National Gallery perhaps?'

'I need to inspect a wind-farm project in Dorset, with a view to sponsorship.'

'Art. Ecology. Is there no end to your philanthropy?'

'No end at all,' I said. 'It even extends to self-sufficient smallholders.'

Anna laughed, a warm laugh. 'I'm not sure philanthropy's the word I would use to describe that. Unless self-interest has changed its meaning.'

'It has. Haven't you noticed? Self-interest is always for someone else's benefit now.'

'I rather feared it was.'

'Do you want to give me your number?'

'I'll give you my email address,' said Anna. She wrote it down for me in large, straggly writing. I peered at it to make sure I could read it.

'Will I end up in your junk mail?' I asked.

'My software will decide that. It has excellent judgement. Much better than mine.'

'What's the use-by date on spam?'

'Before the date of manufacture, I should think,' said Anna.

We left The Fine Line slowly, walking down Bow Churchyard in the direction of Mansion House tube station, stepping past the detritus of the day's traders. It was a chilly evening for September. We pulled our coats more tightly about us, turned our collars up against the autumn air, two soldiers from the Great War, gazing warily over our respective trenches, eyes on no man's land, waiting for a whistle to blow us over the top. Or a grenade.

'I think we're going in different directions now,' I said, when we were inside the station.

'Yes,' said Anna. 'We are. I go this way.' She darted towards the westbound stairs before I had time to think of something smart, or something tender.

5

'We're going to Aunt Lucy's in a fortnight,' said Judy. 'She's invited us to stay for the weekend.'

My first feeling was one of irritation. It doesn't take much to irritate me when I'm at home these days. By mutual consent, Judy is in charge of our social arrangements. I graciously make myself available on specified occasions, of which weekends are one, and Judy acts as diary secretary. She is supposed to go through a nominal consultation process, and once upon a time she did. Now she announces unilateral policy initiatives like a government spokeswoman.

Lucy is her aunt, not mine. She is a disagreeable old bag — an assessment from which Judy does not dissent — whose sole virtues are substantial wealth, a lack of children, old age and chronic ill health. So she does need to be visited, but as seldom as is consistent with our apparent concern for her. The fact that we don't need her money is beside the point. This has become a challenge to see if we can get it, and prise it away from the cats, dogs and other quadrupeds that

Aunt Lucy believes, not unreasonably, love her more than any human being.

'Sorry,' I said. 'Can't do it.'

'Why not?'

'I've got to go to Dorset.'

'Oh. Really? What's in Dorset?'

'One of my whores.'

That had once been a good joke, and a useful one. When we were first married and I came home from work unexpectedly late, that was the excuse I gave. Since it was untrue, and Judy knew it was untrue, it was funny. When it became true, it was such an established joke that Judy still found it funny, and I was spared the inconvenience of lying. At some point Judy ceased to find it funny, and I never liked to enquire whether that was because the joke had become stale, or because she had started to suspect I might be telling the truth. To have stopped using the line would have drawn unwanted attention to the subject, so I continued to trot it out, and Judy continued to find it annoying. Her attitude changed again, a few years ago, and again I don't know why. Either my claim had lost credibility with age, or Judy had become indifferent as to whether it was true or not. These days she usually ignored the remark, but not today.

'Matthew, will you please stop saying that. It's not funny.'

'Oh all right. If you insist.'

'Why do you have to go to Dorset?'

'If you remember, we're considering the sponsorship of a wind-farm project. Rupert wants me to run my eye over it.'

'It seems a funny time for a business meeting. At the weekend.'

'The people involved in the project have other jobs. I can't see them together except at a weekend.'

'I see. I think you might have told me sooner.'

'It slipped my mind. Why don't you go to Aunt Lucy on your own? It's you she wants to see.'

'I don't think she wants to see anyone, except to find fault with them,' said Judy. 'Perhaps I'd better go, now I've said I will. We don't want the old bat taking umbrage.'

The wind-farm meeting had taken place a couple of weeks earlier. I had gone down by train on a Tuesday and come back the same day. I hadn't told Judy. I needed the pretext for my visit to Anna, and it needed to be for a weekend. It had been a month since the encounter at Tate Modern. An uneventful month. Lehman Brothers had gone bust. RBS and Lloyd's had been bailed out. The world's financial system had collapsed. Nothing much had happened.

I felt terrific about the brouhaha. Thank goodness I didn't still have a job, I thought. I watched Rupert Loxley and the other directors run around like headless chickens, summoning emergency board meetings, cancelling them, rescheduling them, and decided I was well out of it. Because I was detached, my views were constantly sought. Even Rupert swallowed his pride and asked for my advice. I said I would need to charge a consultancy fee. It was meant as a joke. Bugger me, he agreed.

People like the occasional crisis. Crises create adrenalin. They relieve boredom. They make people think that something matters, that they matter. There's always a sense of anticlimax when crises end. My advice may have been sought, but it was not taken. It insulted their egos. There was nothing any of them could do. They were bits of balsa wood in a hurricane. I advised locking the doors for a few weeks and going on holiday. That was not what they wanted to hear. They wanted to be told that their input would be of crucial importance, that they alone, by doing the right thing at the right time, could avert Armageddon. God, we're all so stupid.

During that month, I made no attempt to contact Anna. I told myself that I was playing it cool, which was what I told myself as a teenager when I left it a good ten minutes before ringing the latest excitement. In truth, I was having second thoughts. I wanted Anna desperately, but desperation seemed an insufficient motive for action.

At the back of my mind was a small power tool, attempting to drill a simple and unwelcome thought into my skull: 'You're only doing this, knobhead, because Anna rejected you in '67 and you want to show her she was wrong.' I had, I thought, an impressive array of arguments to convince the power tool it was mistaken, but the drill was impervious to rational debate and persisted in boring me with its mantra. It didn't succeed in dissuading me from my intentions, but it induced a paralysis when it came to implementing them.

Judy's announcement of the proposed visit to Aunt Lucy offered an escape from this impasse and I seized it before I had time to think about it.

'Yes, you go on your own,' I said. 'Excellent idea.'

'Very well,' said Judy. 'Although she'll be disappointed not to see you. Are you playing golf this afternoon?'

'Yes. Unless you have other plans.' This was a symbolic remark, symbolizing nothing.

'I thought I'd go to the garden centre. It's nearly winter, after all, and I really must get something for that bed under the ornamental cherry for next spring.'

'Good idea,' I said.

'And don't forget the Carsons are coming to lunch tomorrow.'

'The Carsons?'

'Oh, Matthew, do pay attention. I play tennis with Jezzy Carson. Her husband's this year's chairman of the Rotary. You met them at the fork supper for the Conservatives.'

'I was under a general anaesthetic that night,' I said. 'Have you really got a friend called Jezzy?'

'Yes.'

'Amazing. Please say her husband's called Ahab.'

'He's called Brian. And she's Jessica really.'

My sixtieth was nearly five months ago now. I couldn't honestly say it had been forgotten. I was reasonably sure, for example, that if I ever reached my seventieth, it would be celebrated differently. Life had returned to what passed for normal. Judy had granted a conditional pardon. My children were talking to me, although, now I come to think of it, I hadn't seen either of their partners in the interim. However, Judy was still not issuing social invitations to the friends present that night, possibly because we weren't receiving any from them. She was therefore reduced to entertaining people who were even more distant acquaintances than the acquaintances who passed for friends. Ahab and Jezebel were two of them.

'Remind me what Ahab does when he's not rotating,' I said.

'He's senior partner at a firm of accountants in Potters Bar,' said Judy. 'Jezzy knows you work in the City. She says Brian's itching to talk to someone who's in the eye of the storm.'

If it was nearly five months since my birthday, it must have been more than four since I'd lost my job. Doesn't time fly when you're enjoying yourself? I had more or less persuaded myself that I was still in work. Somewhere, at the back of my mind, I must have known that I was deceiving myself. Surely I knew that I was out of work and would never work again, didn't I? I must have realized that I would have to tell Judy at some point, that the longer I left it the worse it would be, that those dread thoughts of a barren future would have to be confronted. Hadn't I? I ask, not rhetorically, but because I don't know the answers. I fear that I had believed my own delusion. I don't know how long one has to live a lie before it starts to feel like the truth. Perhaps not for very long.

I had no idea what I was going to say to

Ahab about life in the City during la-la time. When I used to tell people I worked there, they assumed I must be a banker of some sort, as Ahab probably did. I always bridled at the assumption. That had little to do with the present reputation of bankers; everything to do with how I imagined myself when I was growing up. Our generation was meant to be different. We invented sex and music, and freedom and peace, and all sorts of things that turned out to be unpatentable. We invented ourselves, in fact. And we didn't invent ourselves in order to become bankers or accountants, to work in a nine-to-five job until we were sixty-five, collect a gold watch and a pension, and die shortly afterwards. We were not planning to die at all. We would be immortal.

I don't think we considered who was to do the banking and the accounting that we were not proposing to do ourselves. I think we hoped that these careers would prove redundant in the future we were about to create. They had to do with the movement of money, which was deeply boring. Money existed. That was the secret we knew and our parents didn't. They thought that money was illusory, that you had to slave all your life to make it real, and not spend it in case it became illusory again. We knew that it simply existed, and that its purpose in life was to be spent. That was how it reproduced itself. That was why it existed in greater quantities every year.

Our life's work was not to shuffle this stuff around. Our life's work was to change the world and to reinvent human nature: modest ambitions that we felt to be well within our compass.

I've now spent most of a lifetime sitting in an office off Leadenhall Street, shuffling the stuff around. I consider myself a failure and a hypocrite. I have always told people, and more especially myself, that I work as a gambler, because that sounds more rakish, more subversive. Since it has been revealed that bankers are gamblers too, that the entire City is an offshore offshoot of Ladbroke's, it is thought neither rakish nor subversive, but greedy and seedy. I note that our corporate brochure, which once portrayed the art of buying futures as the epitome of daredevilry and flair, now emphasizes prosaic research-based virtues.

This is bad enough. In fact it's utterly damning. But it now turns out that we were wrong about the very nature of money itself, and that our parents were right. Money is indeed illusory. Sometimes it reproduces itself; at other times it wears a chastity belt. It doesn't necessarily exist in greater quantities every year. At times it disappears altogether. So I'm not only a failure and a hypocrite, but an idiot to boot.

Most men like to feel proud of what they have achieved in their careers and are hurt when it is belittled by their wives. With Judy and me, it's the reverse. I'm the one for belittlement, to myself anyhow. Judy is proud of me. I have provided safety and security, a regular flow of income, two children, a dog and a cat, and a house in Barnet with a large garden. My success is tangible — unlike fidelity, say, or love, which come with no written receipt. I can be lauded at social events in the neighbourhood, and as long as I attend some of them and fail to mention that I vote Labour, my peccadilloes are over-looked. This is one reason it is so hard to tell her that I am now officially a failure.

We seldom make love these days. Once a month perhaps. I do not count the days between. Judy has lost her libido, or I think she has. It's only a guess because we don't discuss it. I haven't lost mine, but it has diminished to the point where I think I've lost it, until someone like Anna comes along and I realize I haven't. I can't remember when I last found Judy attractive. She probably can't remember when she last found me attractive.

I don't think either of us is attractive. To anyone, probably. I don't think either of us is interesting. To anyone, probably. We all become clichés of something or other, don't we? We shave off our eccentric appendages, reduce ourselves to a manageable essence, then make a cliché out of it. I'm a cliché of someone who does something in the City. Judy's a cliché of the woman from the Oxo commercial. How depressing.

We seldom go to bed at the same time. She is usually asleep, or pretending to be, when I climb between the sheets. When we do retire together, when I've said goodnight and turned out the light, Judy will always say something, a few words to confirm that the cocoon is securely in place.

That night she said: 'We have a very pleasant life, don't we, Matthew?'

It took me a long time to get to sleep after that. I loathe the word 'pleasant'. I would prefer any other adjective to define my life. It conjures an image of anaemia, of a medication devoid of active ingredients. A pleasant life stops at the second glass.

The bastard fact of the matter is that Judy and I really do have a pleasant life. And the other bastard fact is that Judy considers this a triumph, and I consider it a failure. As far as she is concerned, everything has to be safe and secure, firmly under some avuncular control and with no hint of risk. No one must be offended under any circumstances. The acme of achievement is to be honoured with the word boredom as the cause of death on your death certificate. I would rather die bungee jumping.

I spent much of that night itemizing the elements of my youth that had survived the bonfire of the decades. To be accurate, I spent a short time itemizing them, and a long time wondering why I couldn't think of more.

I vote Labour. The party has no connection with the one I once supported. I still vote for it. That makes it sound as though I long for the resurrection of socialism. The reality is worse. I vote Labour out of sentiment. I vote Labour because I can't abide people who vote Tory. I go to the polling station. I put a cross against the name of the Labour candidate. I come home, sit on the sofa and feel total indifference as to whether the Labour candidate wins or not, because it changes nothing either way. In Barnet, the Labour candidate never does win. This is not democracy, it's *Strictly Come Dancing*.

I am permitted not to shave on a Sunday, unless we have guests or are going out. This allows me to look slovenly without acquiring the status of a man with designer stubble.

Social archaeologists can observe the ruined foundations of a former beard.

I go to rock concerts. When they are held in warm arenas with comfortable seats. As long as they don't feature anyone born after 1950. For preference, I would go in frayed denims. That is denied me. When my jeans approach maturity, Judy throws them in the bin and buys a new pair from Marks & Spencer. On the afternoon of the concert, she will iron them with neat creases. I have failed to stop her doing this. What the fuck are Marks & Spencer doing selling jeans anyway?

This is my personal residue of the '60s. I don't think anyone else's is much different. The smart ones walked off with the brand name. Pseudo-hippies like Branson have made a fortune trading on the decade. It was when the Rolling Stones announced they were launching their own credit card that I gave up completely. What was the fucking point?

The next morning, I was unsettled. The lack of sleep, the angry, weakful thoughts that had filled my wakefulness, left me ill prepared for a ten-round contest with this year's chairman of the Rotary and his tennis-playing wife.

The Carsons arrived on the dot of noon. Ahab was kitted out in grey flannel trousers, blazer, Viyella shirt and cravat — an item of clothing I had not seen in thirty years and which I didn't know was still manufactured. Jezebel was in what my mother would have called a frock. She had a string of pearls around her neck — fake, I should think; we were not that important — and a demeanour that proclaimed that she shared Judy's world view. Don't ask me how I knew. I just did. That was why she and Judy were friends. These people can recognize each other as Freemasons do. I expect Ahab is a Freemason.

I poured the drinks: a gin and tonic for Ahab; a dry sherry for Jezebel. Judy had a sherry too, to affirm the correctness of Jezebel's choice. I poured myself a large whisky. Judy gave me the slightest frown, as if to caution me as to my future behaviour. She could smell the whiff of insurrection like the chief of police in a tin-pot dictatorship.

Judy was looking very pretty that day, I must say. I wouldn't go so far as to say sexy, but certainly more attractive than for a long time. I wish I paid more attention to these things and could say what she'd done differently, but it was something. I wasn't sure whom it was designed to impress.

I contained myself through the pre-lunch inanities, finding consolation in making an inventory of the luxuriant hair that sprouted from assorted orifices on Ahab's head. Almost every part of it was fertile territory, except for his pate, which was bald. It had been generous of nature to compensate him so copiously on the adjacent plots.

'Won't be long till we have a Conservative government,' he said, as Judy cleared away the remnants of the smoked mackerel pate. 'And thank God for that.'

'Oh I do hope not,' I said. 'I vote Labour.'

It was a shame that H. M. Bateman was not present to record the scene: *The Man Who said he Voted Labour. In Barnet.* Jezebel looked as if something sharp and unpleasant had been inserted up her anus. Judy eyed me like an executioner, about to administer death by lethal glance. Ahab stared at me, his face blank, as if I was a species of mammal unknown even to David Attenborough, or at any rate one with no recorded sightings in Hertfordshire.

'Matthew likes to be provocative,' said Judy. She had hopes of rescuing the situation.

'Does he? Do you?' said Ahab. 'Well, that's all right.' His wife relaxed with the face of a soft fart.

'I do like to be provocative,' I said. 'On this occasion, I was being serious.'

'You work in the City, don't you?' Ahab made it sound sordid. I can't blame him. It is sordid.

'I do.'

He snorted. 'You City chappies have it pretty soft under Labour, don't you? What with your fat salaries and your bonuses and your schemes for getting out of tax? A cushy number, I'd say. You don't want to rock the boat, I expect. Don't want to bite the hand that feeds you. I think you'll find that millions of decent, hard-working people feel differently.'

It is generally assumed that the surrealist movement never reached Barnet. Wrongly so, in my opinion. In this argument, I appeared to be defending crooked capitalist practices on behalf of the Labour Party, while the brave Captain Ahab spoke for the downtrodden masses on behalf of the Tories. Something was wrong, but it was far too enjoyable to stop. So the Captain and I set to it and spent the rest of the meal trading insults and accusations.

At a table of eight, or even of six, it is possible to have two parallel conversations. At a table of four, it is not. Judy and Jezebel had the choice of partaking in this argument or of sitting dumb and listening to the men. Neither was practised in argument; neither had the taste for it. Jezebel would have been torn between supporting her husband and not wanting to offend her host; Judy between dissociating herself from her husband's opinions and not wishing to be disloyal to him. I couldn't help thinking that Anna would have advanced onto the battlefield with both barrels blazing.

It was no coincidence that, at the earliest polite moment, Judy should extract Jezebel from the table and lead her outside to inspect the outcome of the previous day's foray to the garden centre.

'Not really a woman's conversation, is it, Matthew?' said Ahab when they had departed. So we had an argument about that too, for good measure. At some point, I think I may have told him that both our children were gay. Sorry, Saz and Adam. It was too good an opportunity to pass up. I didn't want to run the risk of a return invitation.

It was nearly half-past four when the Carsons left. Jezebel shook my hand, formally, at arm's length, said it had been a most pleasant occasion, before delivering a paean to Judy's culinary skills. To my surprise, Ahab placed a hand on my shoulder and proclaimed that he hadn't enjoyed himself so much in years.

'Never have a decent argument round here,' he said. 'Bloody boring, everyone agreeing with each other all the time. Good for you for playing devil's advocate.' At that point, I gave up. Since I had disagreed with almost everything I'd said, perhaps he was right.

Judy is not the kind of wife to have a row in front of guests. Neither is she the kind of wife to have a row in private. Rows are threatening, destabilizing to the domestic cocoon. Judy is a wife to go silent for a while, to sit reading the *Daily Mail* with a pained expression on her face, excessively grateful when one offers to make her a cup of tea, dealing with her martyrdom in heroic quietude, until she judges I feel sufficiently guilty to receive sensitive words of reproach. I don't always let her wait that long. The reproach will come anyhow, but will not linger. To delay its delivery is like failing to pay a parking fine before it doubles.

'Delicious lunch,' I said.

'Was it? I wasn't sure that you'd noticed.'

'The roast beef was perfect.'

'I do hope so,' said Judy. 'I'd like them to have one pleasant memory of the occasion.'

'Ahab said he hadn't enjoyed himself so much in years.'

'His name is Brian, and I expect he was being polite.'

'I think he meant it.'

'It can't have been much fun for Jezzy.'

'She could have joined in,' I said. 'We weren't stopping her. So could you, for that matter.'

'It wasn't very nice, Matthew. We barely

know them, and there you were forcing your politics on them.'

'I'm sorry. I should have stuck to sex and religion.'

'You know what I mean,' said Judy.

'I didn't start it. Ahab did. Shockingly rude, in my opinion. He might have guessed you'd be a Trotskyite.'

'No. You started it.'

'How did I do that?'

'You poured yourself a whisky.' It was no use. She knew me too well.

This was the point in the ritual at which, after a token resistance, I would normally apologize. My regrets were not insincere; not wholly insincere. I didn't upset Judy for the hell of it. I was aware of the lengths to which she went to give us a pleasant life, was nearly grateful for them. But it was so boring. Why didn't we ever get drunk together? Why didn't we do something stupid? Or different? Or interesting? Judy had committed us to join an unspecified monastic order, the vows of which were never explained, but were expected to bind me in perpetuity.

'I think I'll go to the pub tonight.' That line was not in the script. Judy looked at me sharply.

'And be in a fit state for tomorrow?'

'Fuck tomorrow.'

'Matthew!'

'Fuck tomorrow. Fuck the day after tomorrow.'

Judy left a pause before responding. 'How are things in the office at the moment?'

'Fine. Much the same as ever.'

'You don't talk about your work any more. The only thing I've heard about in months is that meeting you had at Tate Modern.'

'It's the only interesting thing that's happened recently.'

'It must be a difficult time for you, Matthew. The papers are full of it all. So many people seem to have lost their jobs. I dare say some of them deserved it, but it must be terribly hard for people who have worked in the City all their lives.'

There, on a plate, was my opportunity. I didn't need to mention the months I'd spent going into the office without a job. I could admit that my future was uncertain. I could prepare the ground for coming home one evening, a week or two later, and saying I'd been fired, as if it had happened that day. Judy would be half-expecting it. No blame would attach to me. I would become the victim of a global disaster, an authentic candidate for Judy's sympathy. If I had made wise use of the time I'd bought since June, used it to come to terms with my change of status; if I had laid the foundations for a different future, I should have been able to make the announcement with equanimity.

Instead, I had bottled it. I had refused to accept what had happened. At certain moments I had even found myself wondering if I might get my old job back, or might now get Rupert's. Recently, I had withheld the news so as not to destroy the excuse I had concocted for visiting Anna. But the deception had being going on for months before then. I didn't want to confront the prospect of those years ahead with Judy, stretching to infinity. Sorry: what I really mean is the prospect of those years ahead with myself.

I should have found some courage that Sunday. If I had thrown myself on Judy's mercy that evening and said, 'I'm in a complete mess, please help me,' she would have done. Calmly and patiently, she would have done.

'Yes,' I said. 'It's tough. Still, on we go. Just like old rivers and slow-moving trains.'

'On we go,' said Judy. A pause. 'Matthew, there's something I've wanted to ask you for a long time, but I've never liked to. When I was ill and you didn't get the top job, do you think, somewhere in the back of your mind, you might have blamed me for that?'

'No. Why should you think that?'

'I just wondered. You were very sweet then, you know, ferrying me to all the hospital appointments and sitting with me and everything. But it must have taken quite a toll on you. It didn't come at a very good time for you, did it?'

'I suppose not,' I said. 'But it was horrible for you, most of all. Anyway, whatever happened, happened. Who knows all the ins and outs of it. But I don't hold it against you, no. I'm sure I don't.'

Another long pause.

'I was thinking it would be nice to have a holiday,' said Judy. 'We haven't been away since April. We could have a change of scenery. Go to France, perhaps. You always relax in France. Start talking about future plans. It will be on us before we know it.'

'Good idea,' I said. 'I'll see if I can get some time off in a few weeks.'

'Yes. Why don't you?'

'I will then. Well, if that's all sorted, I'll be off to the pub.'

'Are you sure you want to go?'

'Yes,' I said. 'I'm sure. Don't worry about supper. Lunch was so good I couldn't eat another thing.'

Judy smiled. I think it was a smile.

I don't know why I went to the pub. I didn't want to go, but I had announced that

I would be going, and so I went. It was not a place I knew well. I had probably drunk there no more than three or four times over the years. It was almost deserted on a Sunday night. A couple of young men played pinball in the corner. The landlord had taken the night off. Behind the bar was a boy who can barely have been over the legal age. The sound system played what I have learned to call R&B, although it isn't.

It wasn't a happy evening. I don't think I'd appreciated how much I must have changed in recent years. To me, I was the same as I'd always been. A bit more crotchety, perhaps. A heavier drinker, certainly. More depressed about life, well inevitably. But only different in small degrees. Otherwise the same as ever. That wasn't how Saz and Adam saw it. It wasn't how bloody Rupert Loxley saw it. Now it was clear it wasn't how Judy saw it either. I suppose they might all have been wrong, but it seemed more likely that I was.

I must have changed. And now I would have to change again. On that, all of us could agree. I couldn't go on like this for much longer.

Judy had held out a path to the future and it was tempting. I felt like a holiday in France, although goodness knows what I'd done to deserve one. Perhaps, once there, I could find the nerve to admit the truth, and the will to resuscitate my marriage. But I wasn't sure that was any longer possible. Too much had happened. Judy was probably right. If I wasn't spiting her for costing me the only job I wanted, I was spiting her for something. I couldn't think of any other reason. That thought had never occurred to me before.

Maybe we had simply run our course, in any event. Judy didn't appear to be thinking that she'd be better off without me, but perhaps she should have been. I don't think I'm good for anyone at the moment. I can't help myself, so how can I help anyone else? I should think everyone would be better off without me. Anna included, probably. I was a miserable old git and that was the fact of the matter.

At some point everything would get sorted out. The office would get sorted out. Judy would get sorted out. My drinking would get sorted out. My future would get sorted out. I would get sorted out.

But nothing could be sorted out until I had been to Somerset.

I didn't have a good feeling about Somerset now. I wished Anna had come back into my life at some other moment, when I was feeling stronger, more positive about myself. A lack of confidence smells like a dead rat. I needed to be someone who was exciting to know, not some half-cut deadbeat who had achieved fuck all in his life and now never would.

I drank three pints of bitter, slowly, making them last an hour each, and I wandered home alone. Judy was asleep.

6

The sheets on the bed were white, and of linen. They curled around me, touching me like a lover. A matte morning light percolated through chintz curtains. I rose and drew them. It was the first day of the rest of my life, as the slogan painted on my faculty wall used to say.

I took my time that morning, the morning of the day I went to visit Anna. When was that? It must have been yesterday, I think. There was to be no eruption from the bedclothes, no panic and pandemonium in the bathroom. It was a day for lethargic movement, for fastidiousness in preparation, for the crystalline examination of each second.

I was the man with no job on his way to a meeting. I was the man with no income who awoke in a luxury hotel room. I was the black-tied gambler with pebbles in his pockets. I was a supplicant for the alms of a stranger who was not a stranger. To take these disparate elements, to transform them, to substantiate them, to make them into something beyond the nebulous bric-a-brac they were, was the business of the day.

I had sent Anna an email from my virtual computer, placed on my virtual desk, housed in my virtual office, a fortnight earlier, the day after the lunch with Ahab and Jezebel. 'Hi, Anna,' I wrote — I was used to hi-ing; it made me sound young, casual. 'Hi, Anna,' and then the rigmarole, artfully composed to sound artless on the Northern Line that morning. 'Great to meet you . . . remember the meeting I told you about? . . . I'll be in Dorset on Friday week . . . thought I might pop over to see you on the Saturday morning.'

'Dear Matthew,' she had replied. 'Amazingly, I appear to be free. I'm usually on a stall at the farmers' market on Saturdays, but there isn't one that day. Why don't you aim to come at about 11 and I'll give you lunch.' She sent directions. No map, just arcane references to roads unnamed and unnumbered, to a barn without a roof, to the third gate on the left: mandated stepping stones on a route to Middle-earth, each spaced an inch further than a man's stride.

My plan was provisional. It may give the impression of an orthodox military campaign: identify the first objective; seize it; move on to the second. Carry on, Sergeant Major. Very good, sir. That sort of stuff. That was how it had started. Now it needed to become mobile, to embrace lightning strikes across open terrain and tactical withdrawals to the woods, or whatever it is people do when they fight wars. Provisionally I would have lunch with Anna. Provisionally we would go for a walk, using up as much of the afternoon as possible. Provisionally I would ask her out to dinner. Provisionally we would return to her cottage, quite late, quite loosened by the wine. Provisionally we would . . . we would . . . no, mustn't get carried away.

Does this sound premeditated? I may be contradicting myself. I may not have the flair for mobile warfare and I don't know why. I should be trained for it. For all those years, I sat at a desk and appeared to make money by guessing. But it wasn't guesswork, because you cannot guess for nearly forty years and end up anything much better than evens. And it wasn't research, or not very much research. It started with intuition and, over time, intuition came to be partnered by experience, and both came to be partnered by improvisation. Which was how this day needed to be, how it could not be for some reason.

I started trading futures for a bet, for a laugh, for ha-ha-ha. At university, none of us planned a career in the City, surprise surprise. We would be journalists, or poets, or teachers. Something useful. Something that didn't demand a suit or a haircut. We would choose vantage points, the commanding heights of our autonomy, from which to undermine the status quo. One night in the bar, several pints into the barrel, someone spun a riff about the joke it would be if we all got suits and haircuts, went for interviews at merchant banks and did the undermining from within. At half-past eleven at night, with a bellyful of beer, it seemed a riotous idea. I said I'd do it. Someone bet me a fiver I wouldn't. Then we all thought we'd do it. That's how it started.

Nowadays I look at each year's sprouting of graduates, and they are peas from a different pod, or from the same pod, to put it another way. They are neat and tidy, eager to impress, like lemmings volunteering for a cliff-side patrol. Jump through this hoop, we say, and they do. Wiggle your ears while you touch your toes, we say, and they do. We award some of them a passport to the future. To the rest we say fuck off. It was different once. There were more jobs than there were of us. We were the ones at the interviews saying show us what you can do, show us why we should come and work for you, you fat bastards. We didn't visit the barber beforehand. And our prospective employers were terrified of us, in a way we have never been of our children's generation. They used to shit themselves about what we might do when we got the chance. The only drawback was that we were identifiable. The length of our hair and the clothes we wore commissioned us into an irregular army. That was the brilliance of the bar-room idea. We would go in under cover. If we had dark suits and a short back and sides, who could tell what was going on in our heads? It's an approach that terrorists might usefully adopt.

I was the only one of us to carry it through. I suppose you can undermine a system from within. But it needed qualities I didn't have, and perhaps a system that was less seductive, more oppressive. In the end, I've undermined nothing and no one except myself.

In the bathroom, I discovered that I'd run out of pills. I thought I had several dozen left when I set off. Possibly I took more than I should have on Friday. It didn't matter. I wouldn't need them now.

I shaved twice that morning, once up and once down. I don't think I've done that since my wedding day. And I took a bath, not a shower. As I lay in it, I tried to induce the state of mind that meditation is supposed to confer, without the meditation. I numbered my blessings and the fingers of two hands were not sufficient for them. I told myself that today was unimportant, that it made no difference what happened, that life could become full and fulfilling in many ways and in most circumstances. This was a futile procedure. My mind needed no persuasion; my mind had always believed that. But no one has yet convinced their emotions through rational argument, and there would be no persuasion of my feelings that morning, or any morning. Anna was my talisman of future happiness. I had not come far in more than forty years.

I couldn't decide whether this weekend constituted fantasy or reality or both. As an experiment, I pinched my toes in the bath. They were there, so I was there, so there was some element of reality. So far so good. On the other hand, Anna was not in the bath, so there must have been some element of fantasy. What about my job? That was fantasy, but I went to the office every day, so it must also be real. Barnet was real. Judy was real. But, sitting in the bath, they did not feel real. They felt like a bad dream. I seemed to be in some exalted metaphysical state where everything in my life was both real and fantastic. I expect one of the ancient religions had a word for it, the Zoroastrians probably.

This is another reason why the decision I have made is such a good one. It will resolve the issue of what is real and what is fantasy without my having to do it myself.

Amid the hypertension, I needed to decide whether to tell Anna that I had lost my job, and whether to tell her that the wind-farm meeting had taken place weeks earlier. I was tempted to tell her both these things. One of the reasons for wanting Anna was that I felt I could tell her anything, everything. This resumed friendship was already based on one lie that would need to be addressed. I didn't want to add two more. But was it wise? Did I want to admit to her, so soon, that I was unemployed, or that I had driven two hundred miles with the sole purpose of seeing her?

After breakfast, I packed my bag and got into the car. It was my car now, not the company's, part of my severance package. It was a trophy car, not the sort designed to drive narrow and muddy Somerset lanes. I reckoned I must be about twenty minutes from Anna's cottage, and I had left myself an hour to reach it. I would identify the location, park up and read the newspaper until it was time to arrive. I had ordered the *Guardian* at the hotel that morning. No bloody *Daily Mail* that day. I punched the postcode into my satnav and set off into the interior.

I've lived an urban and suburban life from

childhood. Roads have run mostly in straight lines and the routes from A to B have been uncomplicated. The countryside I know is genteel countryside. Cows wipe their arses after they shit. In fact, it's not really countryside at all. It's an artist's impression of how the countryside should look in the late twentieth and early twenty-first centuries. The main crops are subsidies. Occasionally, not very often, Judy and I have ventured into raw country, staying in agreeable boutique hotels and dining on exotic menu items flown in from around the world, while surrounded by acres of fresh local produce.

This secreted area was a world apart. Straddling the border of Somerset and Devon, it was a sprawling expanse of countryside, with no towns, just villages of differing sizes. Villages with names like Hemyock and Clayhidon, Uffculme and Upottery, which you would think no one could have invented. Roads did not run from A to B, or in straight lines at all. They ran like rivers, serendipitously seeking an ocean that did not exist, through banked ferns and ragwort, ivy choking the trees.

The villages were unpretentious. They sported occasional buildings of blunt ugliness, as if to brag that there was so much beauty to spare that they could afford to wreck this particular corner of it. If there were streets called Orchard Road or Rectory Way, it was because they ran through orchards or led to a rectory, not because some sleazy property developer was trying to pull the wool over your eyes. They had pubs where people would drink beer and cider, not mineral water. I expect they sold pork scratchings that came from pigs.

I don't know how many square miles can be covered by a single postcode. In this case, it seemed like several thousand. The satnav must have directed me up and down every lane in the neighbourhood. None of them led me to Anna. I saw no one to ask in this pastoral desert, even if I could have mustered the good sense to ask them. After an hour or so, I found my way back to the main road from which Anna's directions had begun, turned off the satnav and tried to follow them. I fared no better with that approach.

In this landscape, navigation would have been difficult even with signposts. The old cast-iron signs, that had stood since tarmac was first applied to rutted tracks, had evidently now rusted beyond repair. The two county councils seemed to have embarked on a joint programme to replace them with plastic. The first phase of the project, the removal of the old signs, had been success-fully completed. In a few years' time, they would probably get round to the second phase.

It turned into a horrendous morning. Panicking, trying to read the directions and to drive, both at the same time. In tumult at the prospect of seeing Anna, and equally of not seeing her. Undecided what I was going to tell her about my circumstances.

As if that was not enough, at some point a sign told me that I was driving through the Blackdown Hills, that Anna now lived among the Blackdown Hills. Part of my brain told me that this symmetry was a good omen, the confirmation of a world in harmony. Another part told me it was an ill omen. On one Blackdown, in Surrey, I had lost Anna. On another Blackdown, in Somerset, I was looking for her, but had so far failed to find her. Perhaps I would always fail to find her.

It was hopeless. I would have to call Anna's mobile. She had given me the number, while pointing out that there was seldom a signal at her house. So that would probably be a failure too. First, I would need to find somewhere with a signal for my own. It was nearly midday by now. I drove upwards. At every turning, I took the road that led upwards. I found myself on top of the Blackdown Hills, most of Somerset sprawled around me, washed by autumn rain. There I got a signal, and there I made the call. There was no answer.

I had no idea what message to leave on her voicemail, so I didn't leave one. Instead, I sat in the car, tears in my eyes.

Tears in my eyes, and stupid thoughts in my head, variations on the themes of destiny and of promises unfulfilled. No, you berk, it wasn't thanks to destiny that Anna had materialized at Tate Modern. Or rather it was, but not destiny as in 'the two of you were always destined to be together'. Instead it was 'the two of you were never destined to be together, which was why it never happened in '67. Why go searching for complicated explanations? How much of an imbecile are you? Do you need to be dragged all the way to Somerset to have the obvious pointed out to you?' And the promise, on both occasions, had been just that: only a promise, a promise of the unattainable, not one that would be kept.

I had come to Somerset to see Anna, for no other reason. I had failed to find her house and she had failed to answer her phone. What, a judge might ask a jury, would a reasonable man be expected to do in those circumstances? A reasonable man would make every effort to find Anna's house, and as quickly as possible, especially if she had prepared lunch for him. A reasonable man would retrace his tracks, get as close as he could to the destination, find a house and knock on the door to ask for directions. I didn't know much about Anna's circumstances, but enough to describe her and the bare bones of her life, enough for her to be identified by a near neighbour.

This reasonable man did none of those things, not yet. This reasonable man fell to pieces. Is that not reasonable? Why shouldn't a reasonable man fall to bloody pieces? Why does reasonable behaviour always have to relate to reason? Why can't emotional behaviour also be reasonable? Extreme behaviour, even. I'm fed up with being reasonable. I want to be really, really unreasonable. No wonder judges cock things up all the time. They ask the wrong questions. If they asked what the unreasonable man would do, they might get a more relevant answer. I've always hated the law.

I parked the car in a car park in the woods, on the high ridge of the Blackdown Hills. Thinking a walk might clear my head, I set off down the track that issued from it. It led to a massive obelisk that towered over the valleys on either side. On one side, the town of Wellington, the M4 motorway, evidence of bustle and endeavours, of choices and

113

compromises. I don't know what choices. Mocha and Cappuccino, I should think. Certainly those. Americano, Latte and Macchiato, I shouldn't wonder. Ristretto, possibly.

Perhaps you'd like to consider your options in our coffee shop, Mr Oxenhay. We have a fine coffee shop. We employ a remarkably talented barista. You can have a coffee entirely of your choosing, Mr Oxenhay. You can say exactly how far up which mountain in Colombia you'd like your beans from. And we have five grades of milk available, from pure Tibetan yak to the cow next door. What would your choice be, Mr Oxenhay? Oh yes, any number of choices, but never a choice.

On the other side of the ridge, Anna's side, lay rich, primeval farmland, untouched by any century, rolling as far as the eye could see. Even so, in one of those stolid white-walled farmhouses, would live someone who had once owned a Ronco electric carving knife. There is never an uncompromised escape, is there?

I walked to the obelisk. It was in a shocking condition, fenced off, with notices warning of the perils of falling masonry. I wondered how something of this magnitude had come to be erected in the middle of nowhere. Another notice informed me. It was a monument to the Duke of Wellington.

Apparently, the obelisk had been erected by

public subscription to honour the victor of Waterloo, who had lands nearby and who took his title from the town. It was meant to mirror Nelson's column in Trafalgar Square: the nemesis of Napoleon's army and the nemesis of his navy. It, too, was intended to be a column, with a statue of the noble Duke on top of it. Then the money ran out and no one could raise any more, so the dukeless column was sculpted into an obelisk, as if that had been the intention all along. I suppose Wellington had already become a Tory politician by this point and no one, then as now, would have wanted to dip hand in pocket to build a monument to a Tory politician.

I had a vision of Wellington riding on horseback along the wide carriageway that led to his own monument, hoping to pay homage to himself, being told that the money had dried up and would an obelisk be all right, asking himself what you had to do to get a bloody monument these days if defeating Napoleon was not enough. Perhaps even he had doubts about the value of his achievements, or at least other people's perception of them. Serve him right. Do you think they sell garden gnomes that look like David Cameron? I bet they do. Cameron would look good as a garden gnome.

It was lunchtime and I was hungry. I

thought I might as well find a pub in Wellington. Driving down the sheer escarpment, the road buried between the hobgoblin roots of ancient beech and birch, felt like a flight from fantasy into a sadly familiar reality. The sign that ushered me into Wellington declared that it had been voted 'the best medium-sized town in the South West'. I think I shall suggest to the local authority that Barnet should be designated 'the best medium-sized London suburb beginning with B'.

It seemed a dismal little town. The sort of town that has yellow cellophane in the windows of gents' outfitters to stop the stock discolouring. The sort of shop that must therefore turn its stock over about once a year, yet somehow manages to keep trading. The sort of clothes in the window of which it would be hard to say if they were discoloured or not.

The farmers' market was packing up as I arrived. When Anna had told me that she stood at a market stall on Saturday mornings, selling her produce, a bucolic image had come into my mind. I had envisaged rosy-cheeked farmers' wives selling butter churned a few days earlier, slicing it with wire and patting it into shape with corrugated slappers like they used to in Sainsbury's when I was a sixpence. No, not slappers. Clappers. That's it. Slappers wouldn't be corrugated, I don't think. Or perhaps they would. It would depend on the bedsprings.

I envisaged their horny-handed husbands butchering haunches of beef and shanks of mutton, slaughtered in their own barns and well hung. The meat, I mean, although perhaps the farmers too. I expect they would be round here. And amongst them Anna, wearing a flat cap and brown ironmonger's apron in gamine style, flirting with the farmers, cold-shouldered by their wives, surrounded by diminishing piles of free-range eggs and potatoes covered with earth, or whatever it is they grow in.

I don't know if we all do this: take one small grain of substance and spin gossamer strands of candy around it to create a souffle confection of sugar and air, far removed from reality. Building things up in our minds into grand edifices of delusion. I don't think I used to behave like this, at least not often. Lately I seem to have been doing it more and more. I used to eat candy-floss at Battersea Funfair, along with toffee apples. There was a kiosk at the bottom of the helter-skelter.

The Wellington farmers' market was nothing like I had imagined. It was indoors, for a start. A vast mural of spectacular ineptitude covered one long wall of a Nonconformist church hall. The produce may have been local;

little of it seemed to have come from a farm. It looked like a WI stall at a small village fete. 'A collection of weird people selling stuff' doesn't have quite the same allure as 'farmers' market', probably, so accuracy had been trumped by marketing once again, the authentic by a replica. I watched the ferreting of the women with their autumn coats and sludge-green head-scarves and woven baskets.

And I looked up at the painted beams, held in place by thin metal stays, below a fibreboard ceiling, and thought of another dowdy church hall, in another county, in another age.

I first saw Anna across a crowded dance floor in a Methodist church hall in Haslemere in December 1966. I was staying for the weekend with Simon, an old friend, and was dancing with his sister Linda. I use the word 'dancing' loosely. When I came up for air after a long snog, a girl was standing in the distance, in perfect focus, the foreground congregation no more than a blur. She was not dancing, but standing with two men at the bar. She was tall and slim, fine blonde hair falling to her shoulders. The main point was not the looks, fabulous though they were. The main point was the attitude. She was fully engaged with the two men, laughing animatedly, hand reaching out to touch arms, tactile. At the same time, she seemed to be detached, sufficient in her own space, needing nothing and nobody.

The next morning I asked Simon about her, described her to him. 'Sounds like Anna,' he said. 'Anna Purdue. Do you fancy her?'

'Just a bit.'

'If you can get close to Anna,' said Simon, 'you'll have done better than anyone else round here. Everyone thinks she's a prick-teaser.'

We were so assured then, so categorical in our judgements. We could condense our peers into a word or two. There were no nuances; no on the one hand, on the other hand, or yet agains. Appraisals were staccato. Life was simple. Verdicts were certain. Over the decades, we have applied layers of make-up to ourselves and to others. Silt deposits from different eons accrete upon our river beds. If all of this were stripped away, all of us reduced once more to a word or two, I would still be a chancer, and perhaps Anna would still be a prick-teaser.

I looked around the market hall for her. I was a little puzzled. In her email, she had said that she was usually on a stall at the farmers' market on Saturday mornings, but that there wasn't one that day. Surely Wellington would be her local market. Perhaps she had confused the dates. Anyway, she wasn't there.

I found a pub nearby. It was late for lunch, the lunch I should have been having with her. Too late, as it turned out. The pub had stopped serving food. I bought a pint of beer, sat down on a hard settle and decided to feel sorry for myself.

I don't often feel sorry for myself, and not only because I've had so little cause to do so in my life. Self-pity is pathetic. Whenever I feel it coming on, it quickly transmutes into anger and self-loathing. After a few minutes of considering myself the least fortunate man in the world, I began to rip myself to pieces. You stupid, useless bastard, I told myself. Bone-idle all your life. Presenting your laziness as flair and intuition, because you can't be arsed to do the research. Chucked out of your job because you can't hack it any more. No guts to tell your wife you're out of work. More or less an alcoholic, give or take a Babycham. Shit husband and father. Chasing some bit of skirt down in Somerset for God knows what reason. She didn't want you then. She doesn't want you now. And in any case you can't even find her because you're such a useless prat.

For some reason, I said all this out loud. It made it more official.

An old man sitting at the next table smiled at me. I thought he must be trying to pick me up. Do they have gay people in Somerset? They must do, you'd think. It turned out that he wasn't gay. He was being friendly. Or both, of course. How should I know?

'Hello,' he said. 'You don't seem a very happy chappy.'

I tried to ignore him, but he was one of those pestering do-goody types that force you to talk to them even when you don't want to. It wouldn't surprise me if he went to church just to annoy people by giving them the sign of peace. He had white hair and glasses and wore a tweed jacket and tie. Like a retired university professor, I thought. It turned out that was exactly what he was. He insisted on telling me his name was Ernest. I didn't tell him my name. I wondered how I could decently give him a sign of peace off.

'Please don't take this amiss,' he said, 'but it seemed a bit odd you talking to yourself like that. Is everything all right?'

'I think I will take it amiss,' I said. 'Yes, in fact I've made a definite decision to take it amiss. I'm up to here with bloody psychiatrists. I don't need another one.'

'That's strange,' said Ernest. 'I am a psychiatrist. A psychologist, in fact.'

'Do you have any pills?'

'No. Why should I?'

'I don't know,' I said. 'I'd have thought you

would. Psychologist. Psychiatrist. Psychoanalyst. Psychotherapist. Psychobabble. Psychobollocks. And no bloody pills. Trickling around the country with your bicycle clips, poking your nose into other people's business. Are you trying to tell me I'm ill?'

'No, no. Not at all.'

'Implying I'm one stick short of a rhubarb patch?'

'Certainly not,' he said.

'It sounds like it to me.'

'No. I wasn't suggesting any such thing. Well, it's been very nice meeting you, Mr . . . Mr?'

'Marrow,' I said.

'Very nice meeting you, Mr Marrow. I ought to be going now.' He drained his glass and walked swiftly out of the pub. I went up to the bar.

'Another pint, please.'

'Sorry. We're closed.'

'What do you mean you're closed? I'm standing here talking to you and I want a drink.'

'We stopped serving at two-thirty.'

Something snapped. The brake cable, possibly.

'Well, I didn't stop drinking at two-thirty. Give me a pint.'

'Out.'

I thought about clambering over the bar to get a drink, or to head-butt the landlord. I decided it would be wiser to go round it. The landlord was practised at dealing with awkward customers. He grabbed my arms.

'You. Out. Now. Or I'll call the police.'

This was a fight too far. 'Don't bother,' I said. 'I've no intention of staying in this rhubarb patch a minute longer.'

I wandered back to the car park in a roundabout way. No, there wasn't a round-about, I don't think. There were traffic lights. It was raining heavily by then. I had no umbrella and my car was at the far end of the car park. My head felt a little fuzzy, goodness knows why after one pint. I decided I needed some shelter until the rain eased off. I was by the barrier at the time. It seemed to be extraordinarily wide. Several feet wide, I should say. Quite wide enough to shelter me. Definitely fit for purpose. I lay under it for a while.

A few minutes later, maybe half an hour, I don't know, a man drove up and asked me to move so he could get out. I ignored him.

'Suit yourself,' he said. 'I'll use the other exit.'

The way things were, I felt I might use the other exit too.

I tried to imagine Judy lying where I was

lying and found it impossible. She would never, in any circumstance short of dementia, consider doing such a preposterous thing. It would not cross her mind as an option, any more than it would cross her mind to head-butt a pub landlord. That was the problem with her. No imagination. I would like to say that these things would not normally cross my mind either. It wouldn't be true. Extreme behaviour crosses my mind frequently. I've machine gunned endless world leaders with my car headlights.

I realized that I was cold, wet and uncomfortable. The barrier seemed to have got narrower, telescoping itself into a thin bar. It obviously had some mechanism to deter people from lying underneath it, which was quite understandable, but irritating. It was no longer protecting me from the rain. I got up and returned to the car, focused on looking normal. I sat and shivered in the driver's seat, wondering how to rescue my weekend, my life. I think I fell asleep. When I awoke, and for want of a more appealing alternative, I decided I'd better do what I should have done that morning.

I drove back to what I thought was roughly the area in which Anna lived, stopped at a cottage and knocked. A woman came to the door. I asked her if she knew where Anna

Purdue lived. She did not. I was not surprised, because it seemed more than likely that Anna had married at some point and would now have another name. After more explanations and descriptions, it turned out that Anna was now Anna Halfyard and lived a couple of miles away. Not an easy place to find, the woman said. I knew that already. Armed with fresh and precise directions, which the woman wrote down for me when she saw I was making no move to do so myself, I set off once again.

In my mind, Anna had always been an urban creature, designed for a metropolis. Not necessarily London: New York or Paris would have suited her equally. Probably not Watford, I should think. If I was going to run into Anna anywhere, Tate Modern was the type of place I would have expected to run into her. She belonged in art galleries, in boho coffee shops, basement venues, wine bars and junk shops. She did not belong in fields. She might have grown up in the Home Counties, but no one could call those the country any longer. Alt country perhaps, but not country the way this was country. Something, or someone, had made metropolitan life a danger to her. She had come to this place as a refugee, was now a native.

I knew the roads that I was driving. I had

driven most of them that morning, in one direction or another. I was a world-champion expert at these particular roads. Eventually I found a track that I must have overlooked, or dismissed as an absurd candidate for her drive, and half a mile later I pulled up in front of a small Victorian cottage in the middle of fields. The sign on the gate said Shangri-La. I couldn't imagine Anna calling her cottage Shangri-La. Pinned to the front door was a note, addressed to me. I unpinned it.

'Dear Matthew,' it said. 'I'm so sorry. I have to be somewhere else today. Genuine emergency. Promise. Couldn't ring because you didn't give me your number. Will be back late tonight, if you're still around tomorrow. If you feel like a cup of tea, the door's open. Really sorry. Love, Anna.'

I pinned the note back on the door, not yet sure what reply I would write, or whether I would write one at all.

7

It is a Saturday afternoon in July 1967. I am lying in the long grass with Anna Purdue, close to her, not touching, a hand's width from paradise.

It is a cloudless day, comfortably warm, almost hot. We are in a field near the top of Blackdown, a few miles south of Haslemere. The counties of southern England sprawl around us, shimmering in the haze. A tractor crawls across a distant field. Under sail, it appears, because the noise of the motor does not reach us. We are lying in the long grass, buried in its wilderness. Swallows dart in the sky above us. Around us, butterflies weave through tall stalks of buttercup and corn-flower. Bees hum among the clover. Somewhere, a church bell rings. Someone, somewhere, is getting married. Someday soon, it will be me.

We talk of many things: serious, trivial, ludicrous, pretentious. Not much about our feelings, at least not towards each other. A transistor radio, secreted in the grass, fills the gaps in the conversation, apposite in its punctuation. 'Waterloo Sunset'. 'Night of the Long Grass'. 'A Whiter Shade of Pale'. 'Take

Me in Your Arms and Love Me'. Broadcast from some pirate station, now under the government's sentence of death. We are feasting on a condemned man's last banquet.

I have an oxeye daisy in my hand and am slowly pulling off the petals, one by one. I do this casually, silently, not wanting to make a big deal out of it. Anna watches me, does not say anything. It ends with 'she loves me', but I may have pulled two petals off at once.

I don't know why I'm doing this, because I don't believe in things like this any more. I suppose I believe that moments like these portend something: that they can be bottled, and that the vintage will mature for years. I suppose I believe that this moment will endure, even when we stand up, in one hour's, two hours' time; even when the key turns in the ignition.

I no longer believe any of these things. Yet I do still believe that, without moments like this, life would be barely worth living.

I've gone down to the Surrey-Sussex border for the day to see my old friend Simon, the friend with whom I was staying when I'd first seen Anna. He is now working in Birmingham. I'm in London, waiting to go to university. We haven't seen each other in months. Out of the blue, Simon has rung me. He will be in Lurgashall the following

Saturday, playing cricket for the village team. Why don't I come down? We arrange to meet in a pub.

I arrive at the Noah's Ark in Lurgashall at about twelve-thirty. The pub is already full. People are spilling out across the road and onto the playing field. Simon is amongst them, beer glass in hand, not about to let the athletic requirements of the afternoon stand in the way of a liquid lunch. We drink and chat, and chat and drink, for an hour or more. Then I see Anna in the distance.

'That's Anna Purdue, isn't it?'

'Yes,' says Simon. 'Not the first time you've asked about her, is it? Still fancy her?'

I smile.

'Come over. I'll introduce you.' We walk twenty or thirty paces across the mown grass. Simon throws his arms around Anna and kisses her.

'To what do I owe this pleasure?' asks Anna.

'Not to me,' says Simon. 'I'd run a mile from you. To him. This is my old mate, Matthew. He's hopelessly in love with you. At least, I've told him it's hopeless.'

'Idiot,' says Anna, to one or other of us.

'I've got to go and get changed,' says Simon. He wanders towards the pavilion. Anna's friends have melted away, are standing a few yards off.

'Do you live near here?' I ask.

'Over there.' She waves in the direction of some trees. 'Are you really in love with me?'

'Madly.'

'Oh good. I like it when people fall in love with me. Especially when I don't know them.'

'And when you do?'

'Not so much. They always disappoint. Have we met before?'

'I saw you at Simon's dance,' I say. 'I was staying with him.'

'Did we talk?'

'Wouldn't you have remembered if we had?'

'The only thing I remember about that evening was that two men were chasing me and I didn't want either of them. So I spent most of the time at the bar with them both. Which was the worst of both worlds. And I think I may have been a little tipsy. Sorry.'

'It's all right,' I say. 'We didn't talk. You seemed rather engrossed with them. I didn't like to interrupt.'

'A loss for both of us,' says Anna. 'That'll teach you to go by appearances.'

'What else does one go by?'

'Anything but.'

'So, if I said you appeared to be quite nice, would you say I should ignore that?'

'Entirely.'

'It's just as well you look like the back end of a bus, then.'

'Good,' says Anna. 'Now you've got it.'

I look at her. 'You're weird,' I say.

'Thank you.'

'How do you know it's a compliment?'

'Well it is, isn't it?'

We both smile.

Simon returns to us in his whites. 'We lost the toss and they're batting,' he says. 'I'll be in the field till tea-time.'

'See you at teatime,' I say.

'That'll be boring,' says Anna. 'Why don't we go somewhere?'

'Where?'

'Have you got a car?'

'Yes.' My parents have lent me their Austin for the day.

'I'll show you.'

We drive for five minutes or so. The roads become lanes and the lanes become smaller, hemmed in by burgeoning hedgerows and rampant cow parsley, as we climb Blackdown. Anna asks me to pull in to a short track with a gate at the end of it, securely locked. I climb it first, helping her down on the other side. Anna stumbles slightly, falls into my arms. It is all I can do not to kiss her. She laughs, pulls herself quickly away. We walk with giant steps through the long grasses of the meadow,

Anna searching for some idyllic spot. When she finds it, she dives headlong into the grass, as if into a swimming pool. I dive next to her. We lie on our stomachs, looking at each other.

'How did you find this place?' I ask.

'I can't remember now. It was ages ago.'

'It's a long walk from Lurgashall.'

'I know. I usually come by bicycle. I've been doing it since I was thirteen. It's where I come when I want to be on my own.'

'Thanks.'

'You should be flattered. It's my private place. I've never brought anyone else here.'

'Do you often want to escape from the world?'

'Always. From other people's worlds, that is. Not from my own. Don't you?'

'Sometimes.'

'Where do you escape? Somewhere like this?'

'Impossible. I've always lived in London. So I walk the streets. In a manner of speaking.' Anna smiles. 'Preferably in the rain.'

'I like the rain too. I like it here when it's raining.'

'What else do you like?'

'I like silence,' says Anna. 'And autumn. And the Kinks.' A few seconds later, we hear the opening bars of 'Waterloo Sunset' on the radio.

'You're psychic,' I say.

'Yes. Sometimes. At other times, I'm an idiot. And I like reading. And France.'

'I like those things too.'

'All of them?'

'Yes, all of them. Why do you think you're an idiot?'

'Because I know everything except how to be happy,' she says.

'You don't seem to be unhappy.'

'I'm not. That's not the same thing. But I'm not happy. I never have been, really. I don't expect I ever will be. It doesn't seem to be in my nature.'

'What is your nature?'

'Contrary. What's yours?'

'The opposite,' I say.

Anna is matter-of-fact when she speaks about herself. There is no emotion in her voice, at most a mild regret that she should find happiness elusive. She seems to regard herself with the same detachment as she views the distant tractor, crawling across its field far away. I wonder if she feels that way towards everything, and everyone. We turn over onto our backs, resting on elbows. I pick a buttercup and tickle her chin with it.

'What do you do?' I ask.

'I'm going to university in October.'

'Where?'

'Exeter.'

'To read?'

'English. You?'

'Southampton,' I say. 'History.'

'What A-levels did you get?'

'An A and two Bs. You?'

'Three As.'

'Why aren't you going to Oxford?' I ask. 'Or to Cambridge?'

Anna smiles, a little sadly. 'I wanted to go to Oxford,' she says.

'And?'

'And I didn't get in.'

'I would have got in with those results. Why didn't you?'

'How thick are you? It's not so easy for girls.'

'Oh,' I say. Such an obvious answer to my question, and it has not occurred to me. With Anna, of all people. And the audition seems to have been going so well until now.

Anna reaches out a hand and rubs my arm. 'Sorry,' she says. 'If people like you don't get it, what hope is there?'

'I'm sorry too.'

'Don't be. You'll learn. It's the way things are. Until we get round to changing them. My mother thinks the same way as you, if that's any comfort.'

'Not much. What does she think?'

'The same as they all think round here. I

hate everything about the place, all the comfortable middle-class assumptions, all the
predictable expectations. That's why I like
coming here. My mother's done nothing with
her life except have children and watch them
grow up. And now we have grown up, or
nearly, she raises shrubs instead.'

'What sort of shrubs?'

'Azaleas mostly. And don't be facetious.
She thinks it's a waste of time for me to go to
university. She thinks I should be finding
some nice young man and producing babies.'

'I'm a nice young man.'

'No you're not. If you were, I wouldn't
have brought you here.'

She changes position, rests her head on my
tummy, lets me stroke her hair.

'What are you going to do after university?'
she asks.

'I don't know. I only know the things I'm
not going to do.'

'Which are?'

'I'm never going to work in an office. I'm
never going to wear a suit and tie.'

'You will,' says Anna. 'Everybody does.'

'I shall be different.'

'We'll all be different. And we shall all be
the same.'

'Don't talk in riddles.'

'Life's a riddle. Life is based on paradox.

Haven't you discovered that?'

'Not yet.'

'Everything becomes its opposite,' says Anna. 'So the more we try and change the world, the more it will become what we don't want it to become. It's inevitable.'

She adjusts her position again, slightly brushing against my crotch as she sits up. She must have realized. I wonder whether she has done it on purpose.

'Can I tell you something?' I ask.

'I'd rather you didn't.'

'You don't know what I want to tell you.'

'Yes I do. It's what everyone wants to tell me. Please don't, Matthew.'

'Don't you want to be in love?'

Anna smiles. 'Later, perhaps. Maybe love will come later. And babies. I'm only just nineteen, for goodness' sake.'

'Me too.'

'When was your birthday?'

'Mid-May.'

'Bad luck,' says Anna.

'Why?'

'If you'd held on another few days, you'd have been a Gemini.'

'Is that good?'

'I'd say so. I may be biased.'

'What am I?'

'Taurus. The bull.'

'What are they like?'

'Boring. Plodding. Monosyllabic.'

'Thanks.'

'Stubborn. Direct. Stuck in the mud.'

'Sounds like me. What are Geminis like?'

'Bright, clever, creative, charming, witty, original, modest.'

'You could have fooled me.'

'And completely unreliable,' says Anna.

'Really?'

'You'll discover.'

We are half sitting up now, resting on our elbows, looking at each other. I move my head slowly towards her, my lips slowly towards hers. Anna puts up a hand, ruffles my hair, stops my head from moving any further.

'Not now,' she says.

'Why not?'

'Because.'

'When?'

She takes the flower from an oxeye daisy, picks off its petals in slow motion.

'Sometime, it would appear.' She has also removed two petals at once, and that may have been deliberate too.

We turn and rest on our backs again. I wonder if it's time to go. A wood pigeon presses across an infinite blueness, wings creaking, on an urgent mission. Wood pigeons always have an urgent mission. In another corner of the sky, two crows flap lazily. I think I'd rather be a crow. Anna is in no hurry to leave, and I could stay for ever. I light two cigarettes and pass her one.

'Do you really like France?' she asks.

'I love it.'

'How well do you know it?'

'I've been there a few times,' I say. 'With my parents. To Paris, a couple of times. And driving down small country roads. I don't know. I can't really explain it. I feel completely at home there.'

'So do I. I should have been born there.'

'Me too.'

'What do you most like about it?' asks Anna.

'Frogs' legs and snails.'

'I like the war graves. And Père Lachaise. And seats on the Metro reserved for *les mutilés de guerre*.'

Anna's thoughts seem to turn naturally to war and death. A stunning beauty, a lively mind, a dry humour. And always the melancholy. I wonder if it is part of what attracts me to her, if it's something I have already sensed in the distance at the dance. If what I want is not only to have the chance of loving her, but the chance of taking her sadness away.

'I'd like to be in France right now,' I say. 'With you,' I add, in case I am misunderstood.

'I'm going next week,' says Anna. 'On Friday. *Le quatorze juillet*. Appropriate, don't you think?'

'On your own?'

'No, with a friend.' My face must have betrayed my thoughts. It always does. 'A girl friend,' says Anna. She smiles.

'Where are you going?'

'I don't know. We're starting off in Paris. Sally's never been. I expect we'll do the Eiffel Tower and the Louvre. All the usual things. After that, I don't know. We're going by train. Sally's idea is to get off at every place that begins with a P and see what happens.'

'So she's mad too.'

'As a hatter. That's why we're friends.'

'It could be a long holiday.'

'Six weeks,' says Anna. 'We'll probably end up on the Riviera. Monte Carlo perhaps.'

'That doesn't begin with a P.'

'Pedant does. Perhaps we'll find ourselves a couple of millionaires. I wouldn't mind a sugar daddy.'

'Why? Apart from the obvious reason?'

'Virginia Woolf reached the conclusion that an independent woman needed an annual income of five hundred and a room of her own. That was in 1929. It's gone up quite a lot since then.'

'Are you planning to write?'

'Not especially. But I am planning to be independent. Any job I'm likely to want after university won't pay much more than five hundred a year. So I'm considering other options.'

'Like being a kept woman.'

'There's a lot to be said for it. For prostitution too.'

'Anna!'

She expands on her theme. I don't know whether she is being serious. I think she enjoys developing an intellectual argument for its own sake, the more shocking the better. Distasteful though it is, I can nearly imagine her as a prostitute, or a courtesan perhaps. Maybe it's the detachment again. I've heard it said that men can naturally separate sex from love, that women can't. In our case, the generalization doesn't seem to apply. I think that Anna can probably separate the two quite easily. I haven't yet discovered that I can.

'You'll need a pimp,' I say.

'Are you volunteering?'

'For a percentage I might.'

'Of my earnings? Or of me?'

'Of you, of course.'

'It's nice to meet a real romantic. I'm surrounded by mercenaries.'

'What are you really going to do?'

'Oh, publishing, I expect. I'm already a slave to the written word. Might as well go on being one.'

'I like writing,' I say. 'I write poems.'

'What about?'

'All sorts of things. Life. I might write a poem about you.'

'Don't,' says Anna. 'Wait a bit.'

'Why?'

'Wait a bit.'

We don't say anything for a while. A money spider is inching down my arm. We both watch it crawl.

'Anna, where do you think you'll be in fifty years' time?'

She pauses to think, is then quite definite. 'I will be living in a small rented cottage in Dorset, drawing my pension, digging my vegetable patch, keeping chickens, and writing to the newspapers about the decline of the modern novel. What will you be doing?'

'Coming to visit you,' I say. 'And suggesting it's about time we had an affair, before we're both too senile.'

'I might say yes.'

'You mean I've got to wait that long?'

'At least. Of course, you could always come with me to France next week.'

'What's on offer?'

'Scintillating company.'

'What else?'

'Isn't that enough?'

'I can't,' I say. 'I'd love to, but I can't.'

'Why not?'

'No money.'

'That's a poor excuse. Don't be so unimaginative. Come to France. You'll regret it if you don't.'

I wonder if I will regret it and decide I won't. It's not as if I'll never see Anna again. Whatever is meant to happen between us will happen in its own time. It's true that I don't have any money. It's also true that I don't want to be sharing Anna with anyone, even a girl friend. I calculate my chances of persuading Anna to ditch Sally and conclude that they are zero.

'I'm really sorry. I just can't do it.'

'If anything is ever going to happen between us,' says Anna, 'it will need to be spontaneous. It won't happen any other way.'

'I'll work on my spontaneity,' I say. 'When do you get back?'

'End of August.'

'Shall I call you then?'

'I'll expect nothing less.' She gives me her number, and her address for good measure.

We get to our feet, pause for a moment, hug for a long time, serenaded by Procul Harum and 'A Whiter Shade of Pale'.

Another snapshot in the album of memory. When I drive back to London that evening, I am in tears.

I telephone Anna, as arranged, after she has returned from her holiday, and I speak to her mother. She goes to fetch Anna, returns to say that Anna must have gone out. I say I will call back later. I call a few days later, and again speak to Anna's mother. Anna is not very well at the moment. I leave my number for Anna to call me, if she feels like it, and hear nothing.

In early October, I speak to her. She answers the telephone herself, so there is no avoiding me. She can't talk for long, she says, because she is off to Exeter the next day. Yes, she is better now, thank you. She sounds like a stranger. My suggestion that we might meet up in the Christmas holidays is met with indifference. The unmistakeable message, whatever lies behind it, is that Anna Purdue has no interest in seeing me again.

That autumn, I write a poem that I like and I send it to her. It isn't anything as obvious as a love poem. I hope I've learned something.

I hear nothing back.

8

I looked again at Anna's note, and decided not to go into her cottage, at least for the moment. I knew I might not be able to resist, but the thought troubled me. Instead, I beat the bounds of her small estate.

What must have been a modest garden originally had been extended into the corner of a neighbouring field. Apart from a small bed near the house, and roses growing up the walls, there were no flowers. This was a vegetable kingdom. Beds hemmed by ware boards marched in precise formation over the ground, rows of vegetables drilled with precision into the soil. Behind a tall hedge, the hens were scratching away in an enclosure reminiscent of Stalag Luft III. There were seventeen of them the first time I counted. After that, it varied.

What brings us to where we are? What had taken me from a semi-detached in Lewisham, to the students' bar at Southampton University, to living in a posh house in Barnet, to being a sharp suit in the City? What had taken me from being a sharp suit in the City to standing outside an empty cottage in the fields of Somerset, an exhausted wreck? And what had brought Anna here? What had taken her from the comfort of the Home Counties, from her books and a university degree, from sociability and love, to this degree of isolation? Where would life now take either of us? This seemed so solid, as solid as my job had once seemed. But it was as provisional as everything else, dust to dust and ashes to ashes, a smear of permanence across a window pane that looked out on nothing.

In the cottage might lie some clues as to Anna's journey. Yet I felt that I would be searching for them under false pretences. I had spent hours, and not only recently, wondering what had become of her, where life had taken her, whether she was married and had children, whether she was happy, as happy as she would have been with me. Trustingly, she had left her door open to strangers, and to this stranger. But I was not a stranger, and the life I would be exploring within would not be the life of another stranger. Would Anna have left the door unlocked if she had known that? Would she have invited me in? Would she have asked me here at all? The speculation was pointless. Nothing would prevent me from entering the cottage now. I had been issued with an invitation and I would accept.

I had expected her home to reflect its agrarian surroundings. It looked tiny from the outside, perhaps with no more than a single bedroom. I thought it would be rough and primitive, with smoke-stained recesses and dark walls, a womb of a dwelling. I was wrong about that. Outside was Somerset. Inside was Camden Town, a small pied-à-terre in Camden Town circa 1980. The parlour and kitchen had been knocked through, so that one large space consumed the ground floor. The walls were white; the floorboards sanded and bleached, with pale rugs lying across them. A small wood-burning stove stood where a larger fireplace had once been. The walls were covered with bookshelves, each bookshelf filled with paperbacks. Old paperbacks, mostly. Old novels with orange Penguin spines. On a separate shelf, as if not to contaminate the rest, was a selection of more recent novels. Enough to support a letter to the *Guardian* on the decline of the modern novel.

Upstairs, there were two bedrooms, one with a single bed, barely more than a box room. The bathroom was tiny too, with signs of damp and cheap toiletries crammed everywhere. A lived-in bathroom, one could say. Anna's bedroom revealed nothing. It was neat and sparse and uninformative. There were no photographs, and none elsewhere in the cottage.

This was disappointing, also surprising. Surely everyone has at least one photograph on display. I suppose I couldn't quite say that this was the house of someone who wished to erase her past. Not quite. Books do tell a story. There were a few paintings. This was the home of someone educated, someone frugal and with good taste, but not someone keen to be reminded of her past, or to delve too deeply into it.

I looked at her note once more. 'If you're still around tomorrow.' That seemed an encouraging remark. It sounded as though Anna might actually want to see me. It also made her excuse for today more credible. She thought I had come down for a meeting in Dorset on Friday. As she had suggested when we met in London, Somerset is next door to Dorset, but where she lived was almost in Devon, miles from where I would have been, had I been there at all. The fact that I had come to see her nevertheless was proof of serious intent. If I hung around another day, would it look like desperation?

After the shock of losing Anna in 1967, I had set up a royal commission in my head. It soberly assessed the circumstances of that event. It took evidence from assorted parts of my body, my heart and my memory, my gut and my cock, and produced, many months later, a twelve-volume report for me to ignore. One of the conclusions was that I had been too keen, too unsubtle. Was I now about to make the same mistake? Should I play a waiting game?

Waiting for what? That was the question. I might be playing a waiting game until I died, without ever knowing if what I was waiting for was even a possibility. Sometimes it is better to act, to strike out for what one wants, to achieve it or to move on. No one has yet resolved the argument between the soldier and the philosopher. Yet at every turn in life a choice has to be made between them. A British Prime Minister, Balfour I think, wrote an essay called 'In Defence of Philosophic Doubt'. I tried to imagine Thatcher reading it. No one thought Balfour was a great Prime Minister. No one hated him either.

I felt unable to make a decision, so I decided not to make one. I decided not to write a reply to Anna's note. I decided to sleep on it and hope that things would seem clearer in the morning.

At the back of my mind was the thought that if Anna could play hard to get, in fact bloody impossible to get, all those years ago, so could I. If I pinned the note back on her door, exactly as it had been, using the same hole for the drawing pin, Anna would have no idea whether I had been to the cottage, no idea whether I had read her note, no idea whether I would be coming back the next day. If she did want to see me, that pang of uncertainty would surely strengthen the feeling. If she didn't, my pursuit of her was a waste of time whatever I did.

So that was my decision. And I would have the evening ahead, and the night and whatever subconscious inspiration it might bring, to decide whether to return the next day, or to go home and hope to make her want me all the more. And if I still couldn't decide, I would take a coin from my pocket and toss for it.

It was about six in the evening when I left the cottage. I needed to find somewhere to stay. I could have returned to the previous night's establishment, but I didn't want to. It felt too poncey, not earthy enough for where I was now. I meandered round the lanes and villages, came to a place called Churchinford and booked into the York Inn. I showered and changed and went down to the bar.

When the new puritanism has extinguished almost all our pubs, when the last landlord has pulled his last allegedly unhygienic pint, the York Inn in Churchinford will surely be one of the few left standing. Alcohol will have been proscribed as injurious to the public health and the place will be serving betel or coca leaves or ganja, tolerated because they belong to cultures not our own. It will still serve cider, from under the counter, the landlord swearing to the magistrates that it had arrived as apple juice and fermented by accident. It will serve a ploughman's lunch, and visitors from London and other foreign countries will ask what a ploughman was.

It irritates me when I start thinking like this, and for the most part I don't. Or haven't. Perhaps I do now. I have no desire to become one of those ageing men who grumble about the world and claim that everything used to be better. For the most part, everything was not better; lots of things were worse. From the position of things being worse, we wanted to make them better in a particular way. I'm not sure that I should complain if some of them have now got better in a different way. I'm not sure what I do think any more. I'm not sure if my thoughts even make sense any more.

I looked around the pub and saw a species of Englishman I had forgotten still existed: rough, natural, uncomplicated. I didn't see people like that in Barnet, let alone in the City. Judy and I didn't go to places like this at weekends, or at any other time. When we went abroad, we went to France. I would sit in bars in small French villages having much the same thoughts as I was having now, forgetful of the fact that I could also have them in my own country. Manufacturing has been outsourced to China, culture to Italy, efficiency to Germany, optimism to America. Now nostalgia has been outsourced to France. There must be something we've kept for ourselves. In the EU's brave new world of the day after tomorrow, I expect everyone will be born in Greece, grow up in France, have sex in Italy, work in Germany, holiday in Spain and retire to England. We will die in Belgium, as before.

At the next table, five young men were playing a game with coins. It wasn't a game I knew: one traditional in the West Country, perhaps. Their forebears had probably played the same game with groats. I watched them and tried to work out the rules.

After several rounds, I reckoned I'd cracked it. Each player concealed a number of coins in his right hand, anything from zero to three, and then put his closed fist over the table. When all five fists were extended, each player in turn guessed the total number of coins concealed, something between zero and fifteen. Then the hands were opened, and if any player had guessed the correct total, he was the winner.

I considered the available strategies. The maximum number of coins was fifteen, so the safe bet was to call eight, the median. But each player knew the number of coins in his own hand and, unless he had three, he would know that the maximum was less, and therefore the median also. If the first player to call had one coin, he would know that the maximum was thirteen, the median seven. But if he called seven, the other four players might surmise he had only one coin and adjust their own guesses accordingly, and more accurately. So the first player could call eight or nine, to bluff the others into thinking he had more than one coin, to encourage the others into bidding higher still. Or he could call seven, or lower, and leave the others to guess whether he was bluffing or not. It was a deliciously subtle game.

I assumed that the last player to call would have an advantage, but he didn't. It seemed to be against the rules to call a number that had already been called. The last player needed to choose a number as yet uncalled, which usually meant going one higher or one lower than the range in play, unless there was a gap in the range. Even if he made the correct choice between the two, it was often still too high or too low, because the correct number had already been called. So the last player did not have an advantage. Neither did any of the others. It was a game of pure skill, or of pure chance, depending on how you looked at it.

I made notes of what calls each player made and what was later revealed to have been in their hands. One of the five men won significantly more rounds than the others and he was the only one with a consistent strategy. If he had three coins in his hand, he always called the next available total that was higher than what the last player had called. If he had one coin, he called the next available total that was lower. If he had two, he varied the call. If he had started the bidding, he always called eight, whatever coins he had himself.

This was a strategy reduced to two known facts: what the last player had called, and what he had in his own hand. It disregarded any calculation of bluff or double bluff. It sometimes disregarded what seemed to be the probabilities. It had nothing to do with guesswork, other than accepting the previous player's guesswork as a starting point.

It dawned on me that this was what I'd been doing for forty years. Insights and instincts, my arse. I had played the percentages in exactly the same way. The only difference was that I had been allowed to call a number that had already been called. Oh yes, and I'd earned several million pounds for doing it.

The rounds didn't take long. When a player had chalked up five victories, the others bought him a pint. The master strategist had already downed several, and two more were lined up for him. Progressive inebriation didn't seem to inhibit his success. He could stick to a simple strategy through any number of pints. That appealed to me too.

Do people like this have any idea of their options in life? He must have been in his mid-twenties, rough-handed, perhaps a farm labourer, I don't know. Did he have any idea that he was perfectly equipped for a career in the City, in some parts of the City, and could be earning millions of pounds from it? Because he could. He could do my job for a start. Yes, all right, Rupert Loxley, fuck you. What used to be my job. Of course, it could have been luck. On another night, he might have won fewer rounds than the others. I doubted it, but this didn't affect the point. The City rewarded success. It was indifferent as to whether luck or skill produced it.

It had rewarded me for one or the other and, after all this time, it must have been skill, mustn't it? And that was why I had gone on doing it, wasn't it? Because I was good at it. And perhaps I'd started in the first place because I'd thought I might be good at it, wanted to give it a try, much as Ten-Pint Charlie on the next table might do if I told him that the option was open to him. I might have made that bet in the bar, but it wasn't the reason, was it? That was my excuse. What I'd chosen to remember were those parts of the evidence that supported the case I now made for myself.

Nothing goes in straight lines. If you're a good farm labourer, it doesn't mean you'll be a good farm manager. If you're a bad farm labourer, you can still be a successful City bastard, just as you can if you're a dedicated anti-capitalist. To make the transitions, you need imagination. And perhaps flexible principles, but let's not talk about that. Once upon a time, I must have had imagination.

And you need a horizon that stretches beyond the highest ridge of the Blackdown Hills. And you need the ability to recognize that millions of people can become adequate farm labourers or teachers, but not many can consistently win at a game of three coins. So how can your skill be put to good use? That's the question. This is not your relaxation after a day in the fields, sunshine. This is your USP, your unique selling point. Instead of having pints of beer shoved into your hand, you could have wads of notes. I think I had known that. Did this poor sod know it? Would he want it, if he did know it? What do any of us want? That's a different matter altogether.

What did I want? What was I going to do the next day?

I'd had a few pints myself by this point, needless to say. I thought I'd let the coin-throwers make the decision for me. The trouble was that I didn't want to have to accuse myself of rigging the outcome. The odds needed to be even. The champion was winning about a third of the rounds that were won at all. I'd take the next nine rounds with a result, I told myself. If Ten-Pint Charlie won three or more, I'd go back to Anna the next day. If he didn't, I wouldn't.

He won two.

I went to the bar for another pint. Obviously, this hadn't been a satisfactory way of making such an important decision. Better to ignore it. Besides which, Ten-Pint Charlie was in fact winning slightly fewer than a third of the rounds, so I had stacked the odds against Anna. And any statistician would say that nine rounds were too few to be significant. I would make it up to twenty-seven rounds, that's what I'd do, and if he won nine, I'd see Anna.

He won eight.

That wasn't fair, because I'd included the

original nine rounds in the twenty-seven, and I'd already decided they should be ignored. So I . . . Actually, I can't remember what I did. Something. At some point or other, I got the calculation right, got it to exactly 50:50. It was fair in the end. Barnet Fair, as we say in Barnet.

9

I sat on an old sofa covered with a throw, possibly from India. Anna brought coffee and biscuits and sat in an armchair. She was wearing another loose jumper, indigo this time, over tan jeans. Irresistible.

'I'm sorry about yesterday,' she said.

'That's OK. Is everything all right now?'

'Yes. For the moment.' Further explanation was not provided. 'Did you come here yesterday?'

'Yes.'

'And got my note?'

'Yes.'

'Good. That's all right. I was worried that you hadn't. I suppose I thought you'd write something on the bottom of it.'

'I didn't know whether I'd be able to come back today. I'm sorry to take you by surprise.'

'That's quite all right. It couldn't matter less. It's just that I'd have tidied up if I'd known. I do hope yesterday wasn't too boring for you.'

'Not at all. I went to Wellington and looked round the farmers' market. Is that the one you usually go to?'

'No. I go to Chard. Wellington's closer, but

it's outside my bubble, what I refer to as my bubble. This immediate area. Wellington belongs to the outside world. You have to cross the motorway to get there, and that changes everything. Chard belongs to here.'

'You don't like the outside world?'

'I like my bubble and I don't like to leave it. I seldom do, except to go to London.'

I liked Anna's bubble too. We all need a bubble, somewhere to be ourselves. Some people cross oceans on a whim, hoping to find one. It seldom does much good. My bubble was Barnet, Leadenhall Street and the Northern Line.

'How long have you lived here?'

'Years.' I thought she seemed a little jumpy, had done since I arrived.

'And before?'

'Various places. Mostly London.'

'Why did you choose Somerset?'

'I liked the idea of it,' said Anna. 'As far as I know, there are only two counties in England that have escaped the last fifty years and Somerset's one of them, this part of it anyway.'

'What's the other?'

'Lincolnshire. I didn't fancy Lincolnshire. Too far north for me. So I came here.'

'What's the matter with the last fifty years?'

'I've lived them,' said Anna. 'That's the

matter with them.'

'So it's back to Woodstock. Back to the garden.'

'Something like that. How does it feel to be in the boondocks?'

'Great.'

'I expect you'd get bored with it after a while. Most people do.'

'Have you ever been bored with it?'

'You go through stages,' said Anna. 'For the first few months, it was fabulous. I couldn't think why I hadn't come somewhere like this a long time before. It was spring and summer, and I was still in love with the idea. I hadn't got to grips with the reality. That first winter I froze. Nothing happened from November to March. All I could do was wait for the spring. When it came, it wasn't as good as the first time, nor the summer. I missed the theatre. I missed the galleries. More than anything, I missed the conversations. If I'd been able to go back to London, or somewhere near it, I would have been on the first train. That wasn't an option, or I didn't think it was, so I had to stick it out. For a while after that, I hated this place. I loathed everything about it.

'I loathed it because it didn't meet my requirements. You can't ask that of places. They are what they are. They have their own

160

requirements, and they demand that you meet them. Gradually I learnt to do that, and I adjusted to the rhythms and absorbed the habits. Now this countryside feels like a home to me and I wouldn't want to be anywhere else. But you have to know who you are, to live here. I'm not sure my previous life equipped me to know who I was.' A hesitation. 'What about you, Matthew? Do you know who you are?'

'Good question.'

'Does it have an answer?'

'There's this character called Matthew Oxenhay,' I said, 'whom I've been impersonating with some success for nearly forty years. Naturally, I know him well. He's not hard to know, because he's predictable. He's consistent even in his contradictions. Whether that character is me is debatable, even though I am Matthew Oxenhay.'

I threw my surname into the conversation deliberately, to see if Anna would react to it, to gauge how completely she had forgotten me, or was pretending to have forgotten me. We hadn't exchanged surnames when we met in London, and my email address featured only my initials.

'I think you may be a little older than forty,' said Anna, delicately.

'For my first twenty years, the dichotomy

did not seem to exist. No impersonation was required.'

'And since then there have been two Matthew Oxenhays?'

'That would be one way of putting it.'

'Who at some point became detached from each other.'

'Not detached. Sinews still bind them. Semi-detached.'

'Do they share a heart?'

'No. I think not. I think they share most things except a heart.'

I hadn't meant to say anything like that, not so soon. I changed the subject quickly.

'Did you call the cottage Shangri-La, or was that already its name?'

Anna smiled. 'It didn't have a name when I arrived. It got this one in a fit of irony, in the middle of that first bad winter. The irony has since evaporated. Do you want to have a look around the garden, or did you do that yesterday?'

'I did it yesterday. I'm happy to do it again.'

Anna exchanged slippers for Wellington boots. A type of footwear, an unfinished monument, an unauthenticated recipe for beef: not much of a legacy for a war hero, a Prime Minister and a duke, but more than mine would be. I had only my city shoes to navigate the mud. We walked outside and trod the narrow grass paths between the beds. To see Anna as a tour guide of her smallholding, explaining its foibles and challenges, was not to see a woman out of context or out of character. Yet I still thought of her as a metropolitan woman. She had seemed equally in context in London. The move to Somerset had not contracted her life. It had expanded it.

'It's very organized,' I said.

Anna laughed. 'None of my old friends would call me organized. Normally I'm one of the least organized people you could meet. But when I put my mind to it, I can do it.'

'Presumably it's all organic,' I said.

'Certainly not. Do you take me for some Home Counties wuss? I have a minor laboratory in my shed. Do you want to meet the hens?'

'I met them yesterday.'

'Not properly,' said Anna. We strolled over to the compound. I was introduced to each of them by name: Simone, Gertrude, Emmeline, Germaine, Vanessa and so on. And Virginia, of course. She hadn't yet acquired a hut of her own.

'What happens when they're too old to lay? A nice retirement home and a generous pension?'

'No. That's what'll happen when you're too old to lay. The hens get eaten. There's no sentiment in the countryside.'

'Nor in the City,' I said.

'Have you always worked there?'

'Always.'

'Buying futures?'

'Trading them, yes.'

'And what did you trade yours for?' We wandered back to the house and settled into the sofa and armchair again.

'For a pile of money, a house in Barnet and the usual.'

'Was that a good decision?'

'Why do you ask such difficult questions?'

'Because they're the only ones worth asking,' said Anna.

It seemed typical of her to ask the question. I'd never met anyone who would ask such an absurd question. Was it a good decision to have become filthy rich? What I had done was what any normal person aspired to do, and the fact I had done it successfully ended the debate as far as the rest of the world was concerned.

'I don't know if it was a good decision.'

'But have you been happy?'

'I haven't been un-happy.'

'Not the same thing,' said Anna.

'Not to start with. Perhaps it becomes the same thing.'

'Does it have to, do you think?'

'Not for everyone, possibly,' I said.

'For you?'

'I don't know. And for you, Anna?'

'I don't know either.'

'Well, what do either of us know?'

'I know how to make do,' said Anna. 'I know how to get by. I know how much money I've got to spend this month and how to get to the end of it fed, clothed and roofed without spending more. I know what things hurt and upset me and how to avoid them. Mostly I know how to avoid them. I know everything about what I've got, very little about what I haven't got and nothing about what will happen. I expect to die with the little things secure and the great questions hanging suspended.'

'Yes,' I said. 'Yes, I think that's right. I think that's what I know too.'

'Not much, is it?'

'Less than it was.'

'So is that why you're here?'

'Probably,' I said. 'I've come to the conclusion that, after all these years, what is left, all that is left, are the questions I asked myself at twenty. Life hasn't managed to answer them yet.'

'That's probably because they have no answers,' said Anna. 'Did you really have a meeting in Dorset?'

'Yes. It happened several weeks ago.'

Anna absorbed this information. 'So do I take it that you've driven all this way purely to see me?' I said nothing. 'Quite flattering, I suppose, but it suggests you have an agenda.'

'Why do men usually want to see women?'

'To have long intellectual conversations,' said Anna. 'At least, that's what I've always assumed.'

'Thank goodness for that. I was afraid you were going to say something else.'

'There's a limit to how long a situation can be prolonged by facetious remarks.'

'You should know.'

'Yes,' said Anna. 'I do know. It's all right. I don't mind what you tell me or don't tell me. We all choose how we want to present ourselves to other people, don't we? None of us parades an unvarnished truth, assuming there is such a thing.'

I paused. 'There's something else I haven't told you.' I weighed which card to lay on the table. 'I don't really have a job any more.' I gave her a brief résumé of the previous months. She burst out laughing.

'I'm sorry. I shouldn't have done that. It's mean. It was the image of you standing outside your office and saying 'good morning' and 'good night' to everyone. I think it's wonderful.'

'None of it leads anywhere,' I said. 'I can't go on like this for ever.'

'When I go to London and see my friends,' said Anna, 'they're envious of me. One or two of them have been to stay down here. They look at this place and the life I lead and think how lucky I must be, while they're trapped in the rat race in London, or think they are. When I met you, I thought how lucky you must be, with a good job and plenty of money, and all of London at your fingertips. It isn't just self-deception that's the problem. We deceive ourselves about other people too. I think I mostly learn about reality from works of fiction.'

'Do you read a lot?'

'Constantly. There's not much else to do in the evenings here, as you can see. And television's rubbish these days.'

'Modern novels?'

'Yes, usually. Some old ones.'

'There seem to be mostly old ones on your shelves.'

'That's because I can't afford to buy new ones. I get them from the library. Don't you read modern novels?'

'Not really. I don't read very much.'

For many years, in my early working life, I was an acquisitor. I accumulated a wife and two children, a house and a garden and their furnishings, expensive hi-fi systems, the latest technology of all kinds, the friends that Judy made, luxury holidays, a cuddly toy. I accumulated the inconsequential miscellanea that my status on the conveyor belt demanded that I should acquire, far more than I ever had a use for. I played my generation's game. All these things were added. I never noticed the subtractions.

I stopped reading difficult books, the ones that had given me a frisson of superiority when I had read them with a calculated indifference on the Underground. The books I now bought were middle-brow. No one was surprised if I read them on the Underground. Eventually even middle-brow became too much like hard work. I read only on holiday, and only the books that Judy bought. Camus and Kafka had been consigned to our attic. The bookshelves boasted Robert Ludlum and Jackie Collins.

Other cultural interests had gone the same way. Once, the first thing I would do in a new city was to find the art gallery and a spare morning to spend in it. Now, prints from Athena decorated our house and, until the visit to Tate Modern, I couldn't remember when I had last stepped inside a gallery. When we went on holiday, we lay on beaches in the day and ate at Michelin-starred restaurants at night. We didn't explore towns and cities, or their histories, or peoples, or architecture. We didn't lie under a night sky and wonder at the stars. We were too civilized to do things like that.

Then there was music. In my teens and early twenties, music had consumed my life. I liked rock, but my real passion was for folk music and the lyrics that went with it. Politics had led me to Pete Seeger and thence to Dylan. I knew the *Paul Simon Songbook* by heart before anyone in England had heard of Garfunkel. Tom Paxton, Phil Ochs and Judy Collins were regular visitors to my bedroom in the small hours. Where were they now? Their albums were in the attic, keeping company with Camus and Kafka. And who had replaced these giants? Successively, Fleetwood Mac, Chris de Burgh and Shania Twain. Those had been Judy's choices too. I no longer much cared.

Politics had gone the same way as the rest, although I pretended otherwise. I told myself I had not settled into the materialistic torpor of the world around me, but I had. The conceit of voting Labour could be maintained only because now it was new Labour. I was preconditioned to buy anything with the word 'new' stuck in front of it. I had paid extortionate taxes in the '70s and had believed there was a moral purpose to it. Now, if there was talk of increasing the top rate from 40%, I was outraged. Somewhere along the line I had lost confidence in the ability of politicians to make a difference, or the sort of difference I wanted to see made. I railed at the corporate world, while performing moral gymnastics to pretend I was not a part of it. It no longer mattered how I voted.

So many things in which to have lost interest.

Perhaps the greatest loss was in conversation. Once it had been fearless. I would plunge without hesitation into areas that the wise would consider dangerous, and found them thrilling. I was not afraid to reveal any part of myself and, because of that, attracted similar revelations from others. I never appeared to be emotional, but I was a magnet for the emotionalism of others, unafraid of where that might lead.

Now I went to those places no longer. Judy had never been to them. In fact I had never had a single conversation with her that fully explored such terrain. I have wondered whether that might have been a subconscious reason for marrying her, whether some fear of the toll those conversations might one day exact if I pursued them, with a wife or with others, had not driven me away from them and towards

Judy. Yet, until my marriage, I did pursue them. Then, gradually, my old friends faded away, and our new friends were not the same. They were new for a start, and they were all couples. None of them seemed to have any emotional curiosity or depth or, if they once had, they'd forsaken them. The women wanted to talk about children and schools, the men about business and football, and if I had dared to ask them about their lives and their feelings they would have wondered why, what I was trying to suggest. So the conversations changed. Life dumbed down. And the better part of what life was about, or had been about, took its leave and was absent.

That was why Anna mattered. She mattered because she had once encapsulated everything that had seemed important and, so far as I could tell, she still did. She mattered because I had once been in love with her and, so far as I could tell, I still was. She mattered because she seemed, at this moment, to be the only person I knew who provided any tangible proof of the person I had once been.

A large tabby cat melted into the room, its tail in the air, and deposited itself on Anna's lap.

'This is F Puss,' she said.

'I won't ask what the F stands for.'

'I couldn't tell you. It was the name of

Hemingway's cat in Paris, so you would need to ask him. Personally, I don't think it stands for what you think it does. F Puss could be a Frédéric, or a François, but probably a Frank, I'd say. Americans don't do foreign cultures. I think Hemingway had a rather formal, old-fashioned cat, which thought it inappropriate to be on first-name terms with a stranger. I don't think you would *tutoie* Hemingway's cat.'

'Hemingway would not have been a stranger.'

'Everyone's a stranger to a cat.'

'So when you said that in some respects you lived alone and in others you didn't, were you referring to F Puss?'

'Yes. And the hens.'

'Why did you leave London?'

'Why did I leave London? Well, the fact is that I was fucked up, not to put too fine a point upon it. Something happened to me in 1967. It doesn't matter what it was. It wasn't very nice. It sounds pathetic to say that it changed everything, but it did.'

This was another conclusion I had reached at the time. There had seemed no explanation for how Anna had behaved towards me, other than the intervention of a dramatic event in her life. I felt relieved when she told me that. It lessened my sense of rejection. And I felt that I was slowly starting to fill in the missing colours of Anna's life.

'Why should it sound pathetic?' I asked.

'Because I hate the blame culture, where everything that happens to you is someone else's fault. It's not just that it's unattractive. It perpetuates everything that's negative about your life. You end up putting some event from the past in charge, and you can't get your life back again. The event controls you. Everything is the fault of the event. I could behave as stupidly as I liked, and by God I did, and none of it was my fault because it was the fault of the event. And yet . . . '

Her voice trailed away. She sat, eyes beyond the window, stroking F Puss in an absent-minded way.

'And yet, if that thing hadn't happened, none of the rest would have happened, in as far as you can make such a statement. So, to that extent, it was the fault of the event.'

Another pause. F Puss purred encouragingly. 'I'm sorry. I'm not explaining it very well.'

'What happened afterwards?'

'At the time, I was about to go to university. I felt really happy about life, better than I've ever felt. Positive. Confident. Over-confident probably. Full of the things I was about to do then and later. A curtain came down. Instead of being alive, I felt dead. Nothing was any fun. I had no ambition. I didn't eat properly. I couldn't concentrate. I drank too much; screwed around too much; did drugs. I hated every minute of university.

'I had no idea what I wanted to do afterwards, so I went into advertising. It wasn't a great job. I was a glorified secretary really, but it was supposedly a start. Or it should have been a start. I must have done all right at it. But it bored me. I did it for about four years and then I quit. That was a completely stupid thing to do. I don't like regrets any more than I like blame, but I regret that. It turned out that the job was the only thing that had given my life structure, that had kept me on the rails. Without it, I was sunk. I didn't work for more than a year.'

'How could you afford to live?'

I wasn't sure I wanted to hear the answer to that question. In '67, Anna had advocated the merits of being a kept woman, or even a prostitute. I had assumed that she was being provocative, that we were sharing a joke. Many assumptions about that conversation had since needed to be deconstructed.

'I was living with someone at the time. He was earning decent money. I wasn't in love with him. It wasn't going anywhere. I was

174

planning to leave him. It was a toss-up whether I left him first, or left the job. I left the job. Somehow it never occurred to me that this might make it impossible to leave him. I don't know what I thought. Probably that money grew on trees, for a start. I suppose we all did. It always had.

'Anyway, that was how it started. It got a lot worse from there. Perhaps it had nothing to do with what happened in '67. Perhaps that's my excuse. What's yours?'

As Anna asked that question, I found myself thinking of Cardinal Newman's *Apologia Pro Vita Sua*: his defence of his own life. Perhaps this is the point we all reach in the end: to be asked to explain, to defend, to excuse, to apologize for the lives we have led. No matter what we achieve, a gimlet prosecutor is at hand to point out deficiencies and contradictions, to expose the compromises we have honeyed so subtly, to demand an absolute defence.

In the days when my parents used to drag me to church, I once heard a sermon on the sins of commission and omission. Most of us, the preacher opined, would be unlikely to commit many serious sins. We had comfortable lives, in a comfortable country, in comfortable times. We would be unlikely to steal, to do murder. The less the necessity for sins of commission, the preacher said, the greater the opportunity for sins of omission. Those were the ones that should concern us if we sought redemption.

I have spent my life omitting to do things I might have done. I'm not alone in this. Most of my generation has done the same thing. We have omitted to do almost everything good that we set out to do. Now Anna was asking me to excuse the sum of my omissions.

'I don't know,' I said. 'I'm not sure I've got an excuse. Not for my working life, anyway. I've never been able to work out how I ended up in the City.' I told her about the bet. I also told her that I was no longer sure there had ever been such a bet. Or, if there had been, that it was a sufficient explanation for my choice. Would I really have based my career on a drunken evening in the bar and a bet of a fiver?

'Why not?' said Anna. 'I've done far worse. It sounds plausible to me.'

'I don't know,' I said. 'I was thinking about all this last night. Something else happened at the same time. That April, my brother died. 11th April 1970. It must have been a week or two later that I applied for a job in the City. Perhaps that had something to do with it. Perhaps I needed a purpose, something quite different in which to immerse myself.'

'How did he die?'

'In a car. We never knew what exactly happened. It was late at night. He probably fell asleep at the wheel.'

More honeyed words. More elisions of the truth. More repetitions of a party line, hoping to win posterity's favourable verdict. We never knew the trains were bound for Auschwitz. We never knew black people got treated that way in Mississippi. We never knew exactly how Alan died. I knew all right.

Anna stood up. 'Shall I make some lunch?'

'I'd love some. What are you offering?'

'I wasn't expecting to offer anything. But we can have what we would have had yesterday: a ham salad.'

'From your garden?'

'The salad is. I don't do pigs yet.'

'How can I refuse?' I said. 'I'm glad it's not chicken salad, though.'

We sat at the table and Anna opened a bottle of wine. The conversation veered from light to dark, from dark to light, as it had all morning.

When the meal was over, Anna said: 'I normally go and lie on my bed for half an hour after lunch. Do you want to join me?'

I admired the delicacy of the question. It was not a direct invitation to make love, but it carried the implication that, if I chose to place that interpretation upon it, Anna would not demur. I did choose to place that interpretation. I also chose to delay it, to leave open the question of interpretation for a while. So we lay on Anna's bed, my arm around her, fingers ruffling her hair, talking. It felt like lying in the long grass again, on another Blackdown.

'Have you ever been married?' I asked.

'No. Never.'

I wondered what had made her tell that lie. 'Children?'

'No,' said Anna. 'No children. Although . . .'

'Although?'

'I had an abortion once. But no children.'

'A regret?'

'The abortion, or the lack of children?'

'Either.'

'The two were related,' said Anna. 'Yes. I regret not having children. Do I regret the abortion? Pass. I don't know. I've never known.'

'Was that what happened in '67?'

'It was part of what happened in '67. I had gone backpacking in Italy for a few weeks before I went to university. It happened there. And then I found I was pregnant. I didn't want the baby. It seemed an easy decision at the time. If someone had told me it was either that baby or no babies, I don't know what I would have decided. I just don't know.

Anyway, after that, I was unable to have children. I don't know whether that was because of the operation or whether it would have happened anyway.

'The long decline started then. After I left advertising, I had jobs, but I never had another career. I was scraping to get by for years, moving in with men and moving out again. I came off the pill when I was about twenty-eight. I wanted to get pregnant. I wasn't very choosy who the father was by then. The older I got, the more desperate I became. I went to live in Paris. I had missed out on France, for some reason. I'd never been there. I'd always thought everyone should try living in Paris for a while.'

So Anna hadn't gone to France in '67. Her plans must have changed in the fortnight after our afternoon on Blackdown. She had gone to Italy instead. The wrong choice, it had turned out, as wrong as my choice not to go with her.

'Did you enjoy Paris?'

'I enjoyed the idea of Paris,' said Anna. 'I enjoyed the idea of shabby back-street cafés that reeked of petty affairs and Gitanes *papier maïs*. I enjoyed the idea of pastis on a pavement in St-Germain, or strolling down the Rue Mouffetarde. I enjoyed the idea of men shooting sidelong glances at me when

179

they thought their wives weren't looking, of waiters half my age sizing me up. But these were only ideas. They weren't life, even if for a while they were part of life. It's quite easy to fall in love with an idea, don't you think?'

'Usually better than falling in love with reality,' I said.

'No,' said Anna. 'It's better to fall in love with reality. If you can.'

There was little colour in Anna's bedroom, and what there was had leached from it. We lay on a bleached bed between bleached walls, light within light, our bodies the only things breathing, the only things real. The ticking of the clock. The clock ticking. The silken thread that ran from that day to this.

'I sometimes feel that my whole life has been a waste of time,' I said. 'Don't you?'

'I used to,' said Anna. 'Not recently. Why should you feel that?'

'I've achieved nothing.'

'It depends on what you call nothing. Do you have kids?'

'Yes. Two.'

'That's two more than me. I would call that an achievement. Does your wife love you?'

'Yes,' I said. 'Amazingly, I think she does.'

'Another achievement,' said Anna. 'I expect that, if we were to look carefully, we would find quite a few achievements.'

'They don't amount to very much.'

'Your words. Not mine.'

'What I mean is that we thought we would achieve big things. There were meant to be grand projects. How could it dissolve to so little?'

'Well it has,' said Anna. 'And in its littleness, it is the little things that matter.'

Little things like tenderness, like touch, like the brushing of hair on skin? Little things like white clouds racing across a blue sky? Little things like birdsong and the smell of mown hay?

We made love in phases that afternoon, at first languidly, then desperately, then sensuously. Anna's skin was soft and supple as we wrapped ourselves around each other. She smelt of fresh air, not of expensive perfumes. She was eager, as eager as I was, but we took our time. I had waited so long for this moment and wanted to savour it. I felt that Anna must have waited quite a long time as well.

'How long are you staying?' she asked later.

'I should be going soon.'

'Another man who creeps away in the morning.'

'In the afternoon,' I said.

'Will I see you again?'

'Do you want to?'

'I don't know,' said Anna. 'The answer's yes, really. In fact, hugely. But I'm not sure it would be wise.'

'Why shouldn't it be wise?'

'Matthew, if I appear a little detached, it's because I've learned to be this way. I didn't just get my fingers burnt. All of me was burnt. I had to learn to take care of myself, and part of that was keeping people at a distance, keeping men at a distance. It's not that I don't want someone in my life. But I'm scared of removing the bandages and getting burned all over again. I'm not sure I could bear it.'

'I understand,' I said.

'Men always say they understand, and sometimes they do, and more often they don't. I'm sure you want to understand, Matthew, but it doesn't mean that you can. This has all happened very suddenly. Thank you for being honest and telling me about your job. But there's plenty else about you that I don't know. Your marriage, and your family, for a start. I haven't asked because it's none of my business, and I'm not going to ask now, but it does have a bearing on things, doesn't it? I don't know what's on offer. Do you?'

'Not entirely, no.'

'I think I would like to know before we see each other again.'

'Shall I be in touch when I can answer the question?'

'Yes,' said Anna. 'Please do.'

10

What I have decided to do is simple. I shall pull off the A303 in a few minutes and call home. If Judy is there, and if she answers, I will say that I'll be home at about eight. If she isn't, or if she doesn't answer, I'll turn the car round, go back to Anna, and tell her that I'm back. To stay. I'm a gambler, for goodness' sake. Perhaps it's about time to start behaving like one.

I need to know in which direction I'm headed, in which direction my life is headed. I need some certainty. That's what I need. Certainty. No more faffing about. The one thing that will provide certainty is to make the call.

Yet I prevaricate.

I can only assume there is some part of me that resists certainty, that is afraid of the future whatever it may be, that prefers the lantern dimly shining to the glare of a greater light. Give light to them that sit in darkness and in the shadow of death, and guide our feet into the way of slippers.

Another car seems to be following me.

I could make the call now. I could find a

lay-by and make the call. I could manage without the lay-by. Who needs a lay-by?

I wish I could find a proper telephone. There ought to be a line: a fixed line that will connect this barren reach of Wiltshire, or Hampshire, or wherever I am, to a barren house in Barnet. Or that fails to connect it. A fixed line that will tug me in one direction or the other, future or past, whichever may be which. Hang out your washing on the Siegfried Line. Plenty of dirty washing here, I can tell you.

I could make the call now. I am quite decided. Yet it seems unseemly to act on the basis of a decision that has settled on me so recently. Is this what thirty-five years of marriage are worth? I can hear my wife say. Actually I can't, because she's in Barnet. Or on the M1 perhaps. Five minutes of consideration? That is not the equation. It hasn't been five minutes of consideration. It's been either a nanosecond or the whole of my adult life. But it still sounds bad, even to me, the only one to whom it will ever sound at all. So I will hold off a while. But not too much longer, or Judy will be more likely to be home.

This makes it sound as if I have a preference as to the outcome. In fact, it makes it sound as if I'm trying to rig the outcome. That's a ridiculous idea. You can't choose anything in life with certainty as to the outcome.

I could, for example, have called Judy the moment I made my decision, when she was unlikely to be home, and have found her unexpectedly there. I could now delay for an hour or two, when she would seem certain to have returned, to find her absent, gone to the shop for a pint of milk or a packet of Maltesers, caught in the slipstream of an accident on the M1. An asteroid might strike the earth and make the issue redundant. No: this is not a moment for calculation, but of destiny. The outcome will be what it will be, whenever I make the call.

We live in a rational age. We are supposed to weigh our options and make a calm choice between them. What if we can't? What if we don't have a pair of kitchen scales and John Lewis can't make a delivery before Thursday? What if we don't know what to do, if we feel so hopelessly lost that a decision is impossible, if the sum total of our experience and our wisdom is of no practical use to us? We still need to make choices. Random, arbitrary choices. And we still need to defend them, to say why we made them when Cardinal Newman asks us on the Northern Line next Tuesday.

There are good reasons to stay with Judy,

although they are not necessarily the reasons they ought to be. Judy's love for me, her selfless support for me and our children over all these years, her tolerance of my behaviour, of my drinking, even the vows I made to her; I'm afraid they count for nothing in this calculation. I realize this makes me sound like a shit, but at least I'm an honest shit. This is a selfish world we have made for ourselves, and I'm as contaminated as anyone else.

The reasons for staying with Judy are venal. She will look after me. She will feed me. She will attempt to moderate me, will not put me under any pressure. She will care for me when I am ill. She will be my memory when I no longer have one. She will scrape shit from the sheets when I am incontinent. She will bury me. No use saying that she might die first. She won't. That will be her greatest sacrifice. At whatever cost, she will keep herself alive long enough to do these things for me. Then she will rest, duty done.

There is a word I could use to describe this behaviour. I am not worthy of using it. The worst part is that I can accept all the comforts and reject the word that gives them meaning.

What about Anna? I've tried asking myself what would have happened if Anna had not been Anna, but some other woman I had started to chat up in Tate Modern. Would I be in this situation now, driving up the A303, about to make this telephone call? Probably not, I think. Some of the rest of it, I expect. Perhaps even the visit to Somerset. Not more. And what if it had been Anna, but I had not lost my job, was still secure in my own small corner of nothingness? I don't think things would have happened in quite this way either.

This is no use. Circumstances are what they are. We always start from here. It is indeed Anna. And I have indeed lost my job. The interaction of these two things has set a top spinning that hasn't stopped spinning yet. Spin, spin, spin. Watch it spin.

I don't know what living with Anna would be like. I'm now at peace with what happened in 1967. The hurdle of a past rejection has been removed. I can imagine some of what Anna has needed to do to rebalance her life, because I now need to do something similar to my own. I don't know how fragile she still is, how complete the convalescence has been. She has been greatly damaged. I have no knowledge what further repairs, or ongoing maintenance, might be required. I may have to do for Anna what Judy would otherwise do for me. I don't mind that. One element of an old self-image may yet abide in me, the sole surviving element from '67, the image of a man who wants no more in the world than to care for Anna, to love Anna. In her context, I can use that word.

The choice might not exist, or not all at once. If the coin lands on Anna's side in a few minutes, tails I'd think, and I find myself knocking on her door again later tonight, I don't know what reception I will get. In my wildest dreams, I will be admitted and will never leave. Few of my wild dreams have been realized, or any of my dreams. This might be one that requires patience, possibly for months, possibly for years, possibly without any reward. That's all right. I've done that before. I don't mind living with hope. It's living without it that I can't face any longer.

The fact that we made love this afternoon means nothing. At our age, we can screw around as if we were teenagers. When we are young, we don't understand the emotions. When we are old, we think we can handle them. It's in the years between that things become complex, that everything has implications.

If Anna doesn't welcome me back, if she makes it plain that she prizes her independence too much, or that her equilibrium is too precarious to run the risk, or that she simply doesn't like me a great deal, perhaps I will stay in the Blackdown Hills. I could recalibrate my affairs at arm's length, make generous provision for Judy, and stay there. Find a small cottage and rest up. I still don't know what I'll do with my time. I feel that the answers may come more readily there than in Barnet.

I really must make the call.

Aunt Lucy lives near Leicester. How far is that from Barnet? About an hour and a half, if I remember; say ten hours since Judy's driving. Perhaps more on a Sunday evening. When would she have left? She'll be home to cook supper, because she's always home to cook supper. Supper is at eight. Supper is always at eight in the monastery.

How far to the M3? Let me think. If this road is 303 miles long, which it must be, because that's its name, and if I've driven 40 miles of it, to take a random number, then there must be, there must be, well let's say 250 miles to go. No. No. Because it started a long way back, before I got on it. Where did it start? Do you know, I haven't the faintest idea. Not the faintest. Back in the mists of time, I expect.

There was a tractor following me for a while. I gave it the slip after a few seconds. They'll have to do better than a tractor if they want to follow me.

I had to stop a little way back. I needed to check if I'd left any pills in the glove compartment, but I hadn't. I didn't think I had. Then I checked on the floor, to see if any had spilled out, the way they do. I did find something, but it tasted of mint. None of the other ones tasted of mint. Perhaps it's some sort of promotional gimmick. Every tenth pill tastes of mint. Makes you buy more.

When I set off on Friday, I left it open when I'd be back. The meetings would last most of Saturday, I said. I wouldn't be back on Saturday night, I said. It was too far and I would be tired. I would find a hotel and come back on Sunday, I said. I didn't say at what time, and Judy hadn't asked. She texted me yesterday to say that she had arrived safely at Aunt Lucy's and she hoped my weekend was going well. I didn't reply. She wouldn't expect me to.

There's a village signposted a short distance to the right. I turn off the A303. Better to make the call in a quiet village than on that noisy road. Goodness, there's a real telephone box. Do they still exist? I think I'll use it. Maybe it's a replica. No it isn't. There's a real live telephone and it's working.

I lift the receiver and call home. The answering machine will cut in after six rings. The phone rings five times.

'Hello?'

'Judy. You're there.'

'Yes, Matthew, I'm here. Where did you think I'd be? Where are you?'

'Somewhere near Andover, I think.'

'When will you be back?'

This isn't the plan. I know there isn't meant to be a plan, but this isn't the plan. Judy isn't supposed to be there. It's raining, so this should be a day for buying coffee. God has broken the rules. No, not god. What did I decide it was earlier? Gate. That's what I decided it was. Gate has broken the rules. But two can play at that game.

'I'm not coming back.'

'What do you mean, Matthew?'

'I'm not coming back, Judy. I'm leaving you.'

There is a long pause. I think we may have been cut off. That would be quite convenient. What else is there to talk about, for goodness' sake?

'Judy? Can you hear me?' I shouldn't have said that. Should've hung up.

'Yes, Matthew. Only too well.'

'It's not working, Judy, is it? For us. You know that.'

'There've been better times,' says Judy. 'But life goes up and down. You have to expect the bumps.'

'It's been one long bump for ages.'

'If you say so. That's not how I feel.'

'Well, it's how I feel,' I say. 'It's time to stop pretending.'

'Coming from you, Matthew, that's a bit rich.'

'What's that supposed to mean?'

'Do you think I don't know what's been going on since June?'

'What do you mean?'

'Why do you think Rupert Loxley has allowed you to go on sitting in your office?'

'Because he's a moron.'

'No, Matthew, because I asked him. You hadn't felt able to tell me you'd lost your job. You were still pretending to go into work every day. I thought it would take some of the pressure off if you still had an office to call your own.'

'Wait a minute,' I say. 'Wait a minute. How did you know I'd lost my job?'

'Rupert gave me a pretty broad hint of what was coming at your birthday party in May.'

'How dare he! He didn't give me any hint.'

'He felt he had, but that you were ignoring it. He's very fond of you, Matthew. I know you don't want to believe it, but he is. I think he feels guilty about you. He was trying to help you. We understood each other perfectly without needing to say much. I asked him to call me if he ever felt it was impossible for him to keep you on. He rang me the morning he let you go. I've known all along. And I've done my best to encourage you to tell me, but you wouldn't.'

'Do you know what this is, Judy? It's a conspiracy, that's what it is. A stitch-up.'

'Yes,' says Judy. 'It's been a conspiracy to save you from yourself. And it's worked quite well up until now, all things considered. I knew it would go wrong this weekend.'

'Why on earth should you think that?'

'Because your wind-farm meeting happened several weeks ago, so whatever you've been up to in Dorset, if that's where you've been, it wasn't that. I thought it would be good for you to have one or two things that felt like real work. When you seemed to be behaving yourself at the office, I asked Rupert if he couldn't think of something for you to do. And this is how you repay me.'

I can't think of anything to say. What a cock-up. Completely lost control of the situation here. My fault. I've changed the plan. You can't delegate to Gate and then start cheating it.

'Matthew, darling, you're not a well man. You're in no fit state to be making these sorts of decisions. We're all worried about you. Not just me and Rupert. Sarah and Adam too. I went to see Dr Little and she kindly gave me the name of someone who might be able to help. I talked to him on the telephone. He was very pleasant. Of course he couldn't say much without seeing you. He did say that it sounded as if you'd had some sort of a breakdown. You need help, darling. So why don't you come home and we'll see about getting it.'

I put the phone down.

There is a small supermarket near the call box, still open on a Sunday evening. I buy twenty cigarettes and a bottle of Scotch and go back to sit in the car. I stopped smoking ten years ago.

I don't know why I changed the plan. That's not true. I know exactly why I changed the plan. I might not know my mind, but I do know my heart. My brain was scrambled with indecision as to whether to go back to Judy, or to go back to Anna, but when the phone started ringing, before that fifth ring, before Judy answered, my heart was as clear as a ewe's bell on an Alpine slope.

Leaving Judy was never likely to be easy. Had she been a woman to say, 'Well fuck you, you bastard,' or to go through the wardrobe and slash my suits, or to throw my belongings into the street and set fire to the house, it would have made things easier. Any tendency to doubt or guilt would have been subsumed into self-righteousness. I could have convinced myself that I was the injured party, married to a harridan.

Judy was always more likely to do the opposite, to smother the fire with the foam of softness and concern. Or, if I want to be bitchy, to disguise her self-interest as mine. She hasn't called me 'darling' in years; we use our first names.

I light another cigarette, take another swig of whisky. For four months, Judy has known I've been out of work. When I've left the house each morning, in the fresh shirt she has ironed for me, with a briefcase supposedly filled with work papers, and she has wished me a good day in the office, she has known. She has concealed her knowledge like a spy, giving no hint that she knew, waiting for me to tell her.

And she's done it all in collaboration with that shit Rupert Loxley. Can you believe it? My wife. My loyal partner ha-ha. In collusion with the enemy. I don't spy on her. I don't know what she's been doing this weekend. Perhaps she never went to see Aunt Lucy. Perhaps she's been bunked up with Rupert fucking Loxley. Fucking Rupert fucking Loxley.

But there's a difficult question in all this, and I'd better think about it. Am I ill? Is it possible that I'm having some sort of a breakdown?

It's not as if I haven't had the same thought

myself. As always, when someone else states as a fact something one has suspected oneself, it lends status to the declaration. It has crossed my mind that my thoughts have been sufficiently strange, my behaviour sufficiently erratic, that I may not be altogether sane at the moment. But then lots of things cross my mind that aren't true. It proves nothing. And just because the same thought has crossed Judy's mind, it doesn't mean that either of us is right.

I will admit that at one point, a few weeks ago, or maybe a few months ago, I went to see a psychiatrist. It was on a Tuesday, that's when it was. I went of my own volition. No one forced me to go. I should have thought that was pretty good proof there was nothing much wrong with me. If I'd been ill, I wouldn't have known I was ill, would I? So I can't have been ill. I went of my own accord.

Did the psychiatrist say I was ill? I don't remember. He may have done. I don't believe what psychiatrists say, so when he said that he wanted to see me again soon, I smelt a rat, and a very nasty pong it was too, and it was clear that he was only saying it because he wanted more money, and I was buggered if I was going to give him any more of mine, because that first session had cost me an arm and a leg, which is quite a lot to lose if you think about it, not to mention the cost of the pills he prescribed for me, which I should have thought I could get for nothing on the NHS now I'm sixty. Apparently not.

Perhaps I should get a second opinion. No need. I've got one already. That bloke I met in the pub was a sort of psychiatrist. A psychologist, anyway. Ernest: that was his name. Ernest by name and earnest by nature. I spent, what, several minutes with him. He didn't think I was ill. I asked him directly and he said I wasn't. He couldn't have said that if it wasn't true. Professional ethics. He didn't think I was ill at all.

It must have been this last Tuesday that I saw the other shrink, now I think of it, or maybe several Tuesdays ago. I was feeling a bit tense. I got a week's supply of pills, or a month's. Who knows? I trebled the dose, like you do with aspirin and things. And whisky. They always tell you to take too few, in case you turn out to be an anaemic baby. That's why I finished them on Friday. Unless there are still some in the glove compartment.

What he did say, this shrink, was that I was stressed. He told me that! I went to see him because I was stressed, and he told me I was stressed. Brilliant. Of course I'm fucking well stressed.

But that isn't exactly mental illness, is it? Not by a long chalk. Two completely different things. I've spent a few hours with Anna being completely normal. Without pills. You couldn't have told there was anything the matter with me, not that there is. That proves it. At some moments, I feel stressed; at others I don't. When I'm with Anna, I don't. All perfectly normal. That proves I'm sane.

I can't light this cigarette. What's the matter with it? I'm trying to light the filter. Idiot. That's better. Where was I? Yes. Why is Judy suggesting a psychiatrist, when I've already seen one? Because it's her psychiatrist, that's why. She's managed to find a psychiatrist who thinks I'm ill. She probably had to call fifty of them to find one. Perhaps he's been unfrocked or whatever they do to them.

Anyway, that's totally over the top. She'll be trying to have me sectioned next. Or dosed into docility. That would suit her very well.

I bet that's what she wants.

I WON'T LET HER.

I seem to be screaming. Why am I screaming?

All right. It's all right. Calm down.

I'm not well. Let's accept that. I'm not myself.

But I'm not ill. Not seriously ill. Just not well.

Well, what? What do I need? I need a rest.

I need a bit of TLC. And a few other initials probably. DSO and bar. Did somebody mention bar? And perhaps some . . . some . . . some of that. And some of the other. That would be good. That's what I need.

I could go back to Barnet. Barnet Fair. Nothing fair about it. Fucking Barnet. I could go back to fucking Barnet and become a vegetable. Hello, Mr Cucumber, isn't it a pleasant day today? Very pleasant, thank you, Mr Marrow.

This is no good.

Why did the lights go off?

Mr Cucumber is on his way to Barnet Fair with Bill Marrow, Jan Carrot, Peter Lettuce, Peter Broadbean, Dan'l Beetroot, Harry Chard, old Uncle Tom Cobnut and all, and all, old Uncle Tom Cobnut and all.

What time is it? Nearly midnight.

How can it be nearly midnight? I called Judy only five minutes ago. How can it be nearly fucking midnight? The whisky bottle's almost full.

I must turn the car round. The roads will be empty now. It shouldn't take me long. I shouldn't think Anna goes to bed that early. I could get there before she does. I could sleep in the car, of course, or find a motel. Did I pass one on this road? I don't remember. I wasn't looking for one at the time. I probably did pass one. Maybe I should ring her. No, I don't think I will. No reception where she lives. Besides, it would be hard to explain everything on the phone. Better to do it face to face, man to man. Man to woman, that is.

What I'm going to do now is to concentrate very hard. I realize I am not quite myself. It's going to be all right, because Anna will make it all right. I'll be fine once I'm there.

I will drive very slowly. Drive quite slowly and concentrate very hard. I will concentrate on being normal. I will arrive at her front door, perfectly normally, and say hello in a normal voice. And if she's surprised, which I suppose she will be, I will act as if my return is perfectly normal.

I will remind her that she wanted to know what was on offer. I am now able to give her an answer, so she will be pleased about that. I am on offer. And then. Well, I don't know 'and then'. And then something will happen. It'll be all right, because everything's going to be all right, so it doesn't really matter what it is. This is a bit nebulous, I know. But I'm not worried about it. There's nothing to worry about now.

I think the future always feels like this.

11

In the early hours of sometime, I reach Anna's cottage. I've no idea how I've managed to find it. I think Gate must have guided me here, like the one I've just driven through, up the track.

The engine of my car is quiet. In this vast silence it sounds like the roar of a hippopotamus. Tyres tiptoe over rutted mud to her door as if they are sugar-plum fairies. There are no lights on in the house. No lights. No moon. No stars. This night has the blackest of hearts. Very strange. I could swear the sun was shining only a few minutes ago. What time is it? Nearly something or other. I must have driven slowly, crawled like a slug through the darkness. I've been thinking about something. I can't remember what it was now.

Anna appears to have gone to bed. You'd think she would have waited up. I would have done. You don't go to bed when someone's coming to visit you. I am momentarily confused. Now I come to think of it, bed's a reasonable place to be at three in the morning.

I'm not going to turn around and go back again, back to, well back to somewhere. I'm not going back to anywhere. That is non-negotiable. That is not an agenda item. I'm sure I have an agenda here somewhere. I can't remember where I put it now. It's probably in the glove compartment with my pills.

If I were a burglar, what would I do? I would try the windows. That's what I'd do. So I try them all, and all of them are locked. How else do people get into houses? Ah yes, doors. And Anna leaves her front door unlocked. I'll walk in through the front door as if it were my house, which maybe it is now, so that would be appropriate. Except that tonight the door is locked. Am I sure? Yes, I'm sure. The front door is definitely locked. So is the back door.

I will have to wake Anna. I'd hoped to avoid that. But if you think about it, I'd have had to wake her anyway, had I come in by the door, or a window, or the chimney. No, not the chimney, because only Santa Claus comes down the chimney and he doesn't exist. I had to go to Tokyo one December. One of the department stores was running a European week and they had images of Santa Claus hanging on a cross in the window. So the Japanese think Santa Claus exists, which is

203

why he has capital letters. What does that prove? Where was I?

Yes. If I'd come in by the door, I would have had to wake her anyway. I couldn't lie on the sofa and wait for her to find me in the morning. That would be rude.

There is no doorbell, but there is a large cast-iron knocker. I knock on it and nothing happens. I knock again, loudly. And again. Anna is a sound sleeper, obviously. I find that encouraging. Not now, of course, not at this precise minute, but generally speaking. I can't stand women who sleep lightly and who wake up in the middle of the night and say, 'Are you awake?', when you're not awake, but you are now because they've woken you, and they insist on telling you the dream they've just had, which is completely meaningless, so you just grunt, hoping they'll shut up and let you get back to your own dream, and they turn over and go to sleep immediately, and snore deliberately to annoy you, and you now feel wide awake and spend the rest of the night tossing and turning, and doze off at about five, and feel crap when the alarm rings, while they feel great and say what a good night's sleep they've had, and can't remember that they woke you in the middle of it to tell you their dream, or even that they had a dream that demanded an instant retelling, not that it did. You know the sort of woman I mean. I can't stand them. Thank god Anna isn't one of them.

At least I know which is Anna's bedroom and which is its window. It's that one. Not the one with frosted glass, because that would be the bathroom window. Nor is it the small window with a crack covered in passepartout, because that is the spare-room window. No. It's this one. This is the window through which I saw two crows flap across a blue sky all those years ago. Or was it this afternoon?

All I need now is something to throw at the window. A stone. A nice big stone. This one will do. No it won't. That would be imbecilic. Let me find something else to throw. There's this sack here, propped against the side of the cottage. I can't think what's in it. Small pellety things. Rather like All-Bran. I don't think it can be All-Bran. Far too much of it, and there's no milk or sugar. Chicken feed. That's what it is. Chicken feed. Perfect. Couldn't be better. Might have been made for the job. Perhaps Anna left it here deliberately. Women do that sort of thing. I expect Anna realized I'd be coming back in the middle of the night. She probably debated whether to sit up and wait for me or whether to go to bed, and, being a practical woman, decided to go to bed but to leave a sack of chicken feed by her bedroom window so that I could wake her up when I arrived.

Here I am, hurling chicken feed at Anna's window. Nothing's happening. Doesn't matter. It will eventually. It's a big sack. Plenty of chicken feed. And if I do use all of it, which I won't, but if I do, which I won't, I can pick it up and start all over again. I'm in no hurry. The whole of the rest of my life stretches ahead of me, like, like something or other.

I become aware of a hum. And of a light. Actually, I think it's the other way around. A light first and then a hum. It's not important. It doesn't matter which came first, the chicken or the chicken feed. I ask myself if I'm humming and I'm not. You'd think the light would be coming from Anna's bedroom, but it isn't. Perhaps she has changed bedrooms and is sleeping out in the fields tonight. It's a car, that's what it is. That's really peculiar. Who'd be coming to visit Anna in the middle of the night? Apart from me, that is. Perhaps it's Judy. She knows about Anna, doesn't she? I've no idea. I mentioned her on the phone, didn't I? Did I? Perhaps I did. Not that she knows where Anna lives. Unless I mentioned that too. I can't remember now. I could do without this. It will mean a scene. I had been hoping to avoid a scene. Can't have Anna and Judy throwing things at each other. Whatever it is they throw. Probably chocolates, I'd think.

The car reaches the cottage. I'm standing at the end wall, the wall that faces down the track, so the car will have seen me. Well, obviously the car won't have seen me, but Judy will, so she'll know I'm here. The car stops, its lights pointing directly at me so I am transfixed in the beam. This is Stalag Luft III. It can't be. The chickens are in Stalag Luft III. It must be Stalag Luft II. Someone steps out of the car and calls my name in rather a strange way, as if it had a question mark on the end. It's not Judy's voice, but it sounds familiar. Perhaps it's an Australian. It's Anna. That's who it is. How bizarre. Why would Anna be coming to visit herself in the middle of the night?

It's perfectly straightforward. Anna has been out somewhere. Wherever people go in the middle of the night. The Noah's Ark at Lurgashall, perhaps. And because she's been out, she hasn't been in her bedroom, so I haven't been able to wake her by throwing chicken feed at her window. That makes sense.

'Hi, Anna. How are you?'

'Matthew, what the hell are you doing?'

'Trying to wake you up. Didn't realize you were already awake.'

Anna walks up to me and looks around at the chicken feed. There's rather a lot of it. There would be. I've needed to use a lot because she wasn't there. Surely she can work that out. She looks at me in this strange way and I wonder if she's quite all right.

'Come inside and I'll make some coffee,' she says. Why would I want coffee? I'm perfectly awake and so is she.

She takes me by the arm, leads me to the front door and opens it. The door appears to be unlocked. I expect she has a remote-control thingy, or laser eyes, or something. Anna guides me to an armchair and sits me down. She goes to the kitchen and puts on the kettle. She doesn't say anything. I'm feeling better already. Anna's here and everything's all right. All I need to do is to remember why I came and explain it to her. I rehearse my speech and it sounds excellent. I couldn't have put it better myself.

Anna returns with two mugs of coffee and gives me one. She perches on the edge of the sofa, still with that peculiar look on her face. I smile at her reassuringly.

'Matthew, can you please explain? Can you do that?'

'Yes,' I say. 'I've come back.'

Anna doesn't say anything for a moment. She doesn't seem to realize that I've finished.

What more does she expect me to say?

'You've come back.'

'Yes,' I say; and then, to make sure that she gets the point, 'I've come back.'

'Why have you come back?'

'Because you said I could after I'd sorted everything out.'

'That was only a few hours ago.'

'No, it was years ago,' I say. 'After we got back from France. Anyway, it's sorted now.'

'What have you sorted?'

'I've left Judy,' I say. 'She's my wife. My ex-wife, rather.'

'You've driven back to Barnet, had a conversation with your wife, and driven back here?'

'Don't be ridiculous.'

'What, then?'

'There are telephones, Anna. Surely you've heard of them?'

'You telephoned your wife and told her you were leaving her?' Anna seems incredulous, as if she's having trouble grasping what I should have thought was a fairly simple point.

'Yes.'

'You've telephoned your wife. You've told her your marriage is over. And now you've driven back here.'

'Spot on.' It has taken a while, but Anna's got it now.

'Why?'

'Because this is where I live. Where else would I go at this time of night?'

'I see,' says Anna. I can see that she can't see. She's not blind, but she can't see. Funny things, words. They contradict themselves. 'But I live here.'

'We both live here,' I say. Anna doesn't look convinced. Ah yes. I know there's something else I've been meaning to say.

'I love you.' I smile at her, with great fondness.

'Well, thank you, Matthew, but you barely know me.'

'Yes I do. I lay in a field with you once, and had a lovely afternoon in bed. You can't have forgotten already. Your bedroom's there,' I say, pointing at the ceiling. 'And the field is out there.' I point out of the window, because Anna's being a bit slow tonight.

'Matthew, how much have you had to drink?'

'Just a minute.' I get up and go to the car. I bring back the whisky bottle. 'This much,' I say. Actually, it isn't very much. A quarter of the bottle at the most, I would say. That's only about four doubles. Hardly anything. I unscrew the top and take another slug. Remembering my manners, I wipe the bottle and offer it to Anna. She doesn't take it. Nor does she say anything.

'I don't know about you, Anna,' I say, 'but I could do with a bit of shuteye now. Perhaps I should go to the spare room. I hope you're not offended, but I've already heard your dream about Uncle Tom Cobnut.'

'I don't know,' says Anna.

'I insist on it.'

'Is that really all you've had to drink?'

'Of course. I can prove it. This is what's left, so that's what I've drunk. Unless you think the bottle was more than full when I started.' I laugh. Anna doesn't laugh. She's frowning, I'm not sure at what.

'Matthew, I don't think you're very well. I'd be drunk on a quarter-bottle of Scotch. I don't think you would be. So, if you're telling me the truth, there must be something else the matter with you. Do you think you might be ill?'

'No. I don't think so. I'm not quite sure what you're getting at. Are you suggesting I'm having a breakdown?'

'Well, perhaps some sort of episode.'

That would explain it, wouldn't it? An episode. Yes, that must be the scientific word for it, I imagine. Not very threatening, I would say. One episode where this happens, then lots of episodes where other stuff happens. Like a soap opera. Or a sitcom. No, more like a soap opera, I think. Whichever. Nothing serious anyway, because serious things don't happen in soap operas. Or in sitcoms. Serious things happen in documentaries, or on the news. Quite different. They don't have episodes.

'Possibly,' I said. 'Possibly I had one earlier this evening, in the car somewhere, after I'd called Judy. I'm not sure I'm having one now.'

'Have there been other episodes recently?'

'I don't think so. Well, a few maybe. I lay down under the barrier in Wellington car park a few weeks ago. I wanted to shelter from the rain. Only the barrier got narrower for some reason, so it didn't work. That might loosely be called an episode, I suppose, if you want to split hairs. Possibly a few other things that I've now forgotten.'

'Have you been to see anyone about them?'

'Some years ago I did. Tuesday, I think. Some quack I found on the internet. I didn't care for him. His eyes were too close together.'

'What did he say?'

'I don't know. Lots of medical mumbo jumbo dressed up in monosyllables. I can't remember now. He gave me some pills.'

'Did you take them?'

'Oh yes.'

'Are you still taking them?'

'In principle, yes.'

'When did you last take one?'

'They ran out. I thought I had enough for the weekend. That's what I thought. I was feeling a bit edgy on Friday for some reason, so I may have taken more than I should have. Doesn't matter. The banks will be open tomorrow.'

'So you're not on any medication at the moment.'

'Only this.' I tap the whisky bottle and smile. Anna doesn't smile. Anna gets up, takes the whisky bottle and pours it down the kitchen sink. Not the bottle, of course. You can't pour a bottle down a sink. Unless it's a miniature, and even then it'd be difficult. The whisky, I mean. I am now definitely concerned about her. Only a mad woman would do something like that.

'Matthew, I think it's time to get some sleep, don't you? And I think your idea of sleeping in the spare room is a very good one. So why don't we go upstairs, and I can give you a couple of sleeping pills. And tomorrow we can go and see someone who can help you. How does that sound?'

'Most excellent,' I say. 'I wish I'd thought of it.' In fact, I had thought of it. Some of it. I don't want to point that out. I think Anna is in rather a fragile state.

12

I am lying in a striped deckchair on Anna's lawn. The sky is the blue of swallows' wings and the sun has nearly gone down. It is not especially warm, as warm as one can expect in late October. Anna has asked if I would rather be indoors. I would not. This feels like the last day of summer, and the proper obsequies should be observed. Of course, it might be the first day of winter. No one can tell these days.

In my hand is a glass of white wine, all Anna will allow me, and I had quite a fight to get that. It is nicely chilled, as am I. I've tried to draw a veil over yesterday. The veil is opaque and parts of the day shine through. The simplest thing would be to admit that I am ill. I rebel against the notion because I am not ill, and because I don't have a high opinion of men who say they are. But several people have suggested that I'm ill and, if I fight their opinion, they'll only think I'm more ill. It's no use my saying that they are the ones who are ill, that I am now taking the first steps towards sanity. When more or less everyone believes the same thing, however mad it is, it becomes the benchmark for sanity. I've known that for a long time. It's at the root of my quarrel with life.

I slept until lunchtime. When I awoke, I couldn't work out where I was. I looked out of the window and saw Anna bending over a row of carrots. Carrots that had not had their tops chopped off. Carrots as they were intended to be. I realized I was at home. Of course, I wasn't at home, or not yet, but I was still unwell, not ill but unwell, and I thought that I was. After lunch, Anna drove me into Bridgwater. I had assumed we were going to visit her doctor. She took me to a psychiatric hospital, which gave yet more people the opportunity to tell me I was ill. They considered keeping me in under observation. Anna told them that I lived in London and was only visiting. I suppose that it didn't seem the right moment to insist that I now lived in the area.

I had bits of paper in my pocket that related to the pills I'd been on, possibly a prescription, I really don't know, so I was given some more of them. Then the doctor had a private word with Anna about some matter. And now we have come home, to Anna's home, possibly mine, who can say, and I'm sitting on the lawn with a glass of wine. Anna is in another deckchair, looking at

215

me. She is smiling now.

How do I feel? Well, not normal, for a start. I certainly can't say I feel normal. I felt a lot more normal yesterday, funnily enough. Perhaps that means I now am normal, or more normal, whatever that is. Normal is the way we behave. When other people behave in the same way, we think them normal. When they don't, we think them abnormal. It doesn't really prove anything either way. So I may or may not be normal. I do feel calm, though, a lot calmer than yesterday. Someone has installed double glazing between me and the world. I feel detached, as if I'm looking down on myself and my life from an extraordinary height. So high, in fact, that Anna and I are two little specks on a green lawn, set amongst patchwork fields of grass and plough. I can hardly make us out.

I think Anna is waiting to have a conversation, trying to judge whether I am up to it. I don't really want to have that conversation, or any conversation, only to be here. I suppose she's right. There are matters we need to discuss. Many things happened yesterday that I'm not clear about. I do know that I telephoned Judy and told her I was leaving. I'm quite clear about that. I am also clear that it was a good decision. I don't know how I was in a position to make good decisions yesterday. It seems that I was. One way and another, there is a lot that needs to be sorted out.

Sometime soon, I shall remind Anna about 1967. It seems the right time. Then we were sprawled together in the long grass, with only a transistor radio for company. Now we sit in deckchairs on a mown lawn, glasses of wine in hand, an old folk album playing through the open window. This is what life is, I tell myself: this is what it amounts to. Two deckchairs, two Ikea glasses, a bottle of cheap white wine, a hi-fi system and a lawn-mower. I had hoped to achieve more, but I'll take it. I'll take what's on offer. It could have been one deckchair, one Ikea glass.

The words of a Phil Ochs song float towards me from the house. Some long forgotten song of yesterday. A song whose time has now come. A song that talks of warm memories of younger years. A song that speaks of changes.

'How are you feeling, Matthew?'

'Good,' I say. 'Really good. Thanks for looking after me.'

'It was nothing.'

'It wasn't nothing, Anna. It was a lot.'

'You'd have done the same for me.'

'Would I ever need to?'

'I hope not. Not now. Once, yes. Once I was in a very similar place to you.'

'So you knew what to do.'

'No,' says Anna. 'I knew what not to do.'

'I think I got confused when you weren't here last night. Where were you?'

'I help out with a local charity. That's where I was. And on Saturday too. Normally the hours are regular. From time to time there's an emergency and there were two this weekend. Well, one in fact, but it came twice.'

'And then there was me.'

'And then there was you, yes.'

'I think it's fantastic,' I say, 'doing something like that. I wish I did something like that.'

'Why don't you?'

'It's a bit late now.'

'No it isn't. You've got plenty of time. What else are you going to do with it?'

'Good question,' I say.

'Well?'

'I don't know. I need time to think about things. I can't seem to help myself at the moment, so I don't see that I could help other people.'

'That might be the best way of helping yourself,' says Anna.

'Is that why you decided to do it?' I ask. 'Was it what had happened to you?'

'Not really. I think you could say it was a recognition of limitations. Like you, I once had a long list of everything I wanted to change. Some time around fifty, it occurred to me that not only hadn't I changed anything, but I never would. Some things had changed of their own accord, a bit, no thanks to me. I hadn't made any difference at all.

'I began to wonder how I could make a difference, and it came down to small things. It came down to forgetting about the world, forgetting about grand schemes and causes, and considering how I lived each day. The only thing we can control is how we behave towards other people, so we might as well try and get that right.' She pauses. 'Did you really tell Judy you were leaving her?'

'Yes.'

'By telephone?'

'Yes.'

We sit for a while, not saying anything.

'Can I have another glass of wine?' I ask.

'No.'

'One more?'

'I shouldn't have let you have the first, Matthew. No more.'

We sit for another while, not saying anything.

'What are you going to do now?' asks Anna.

'Can I stay here?'

'No, Matthew. Sorry. You can stay tonight. Tomorrow, I will put you on a train to London.'

'I don't have any appointments in London. Besides, you've forgotten that my car is here.'

'I haven't forgotten,' says Anna. 'I think the train would be better.'

'Are we going to sleep together tonight?'

'No.'

I say nothing.

'Matthew, when you told your wife you were leaving, had you thought about it, or was it a spur of the moment decision?'

'Both,' I say.

'Which?'

'Both. I can't explain. It was both.'

'The bit of you that thought about it. What was that bit going to do next?'

'That bit wanted to convalesce here,' I say, 'like a *mutilé de guerre* with his own seat on the Metro. I like it here. I don't mean here here, I mean the whole area. It feels very peaceful. I want to stay here. I think it suits me.'

'So you don't want to go back to Judy?'

'No.'

'Is that wise?'

'What's wise?'

'Looking after yourself is wise,' says Anna. 'As for the future of your marriage, I couldn't begin to say.'

'You could look after me.'

'No, Matthew.'

'Why not?'

'Even if I was prepared to, I don't think it would be a good idea, for you or for me. Somehow I've got bound up with everything else that's going on in your head. I don't know what, and I don't know how, and I don't know why, but I have. I don't want to be bound up with it. I think you need to separate these things out in your mind, whatever they are, and deal with them one by one. And if you want my advice, which you don't, I think you need to start with your wife and your family. After that, perhaps other things will become clearer.'

'Everything seems perfectly clear now,' I say. 'I'm fine. Really.'

'You're not fine, Matthew. You're ill. You think you're fine only because you're back on the pills.'

'I am not ill.'

'Yes you are.'

'This is like ringing disconnected bells on the doorways of the dead.'

'What did you say?'

'Nothing. It's a line from a poem.'

'Strange,' says Anna. She looks puzzled. Then she gets up. 'Just a moment.'

Anna goes into the cottage. I can't imagine what she's doing. Perhaps she's gone to get another bottle of wine. After a few minutes, she comes back to the lawn with a sheet of paper in her hand.

'I thought so. I thought the line sounded familiar. I've got that poem.'

She takes a sip of wine, looks at me, and starts reading by the last light of the day.

'We are the listless ones,' she says, 'who dwell
this side of paradise:
entangled for ever in dreams that exist
to be for ever unfulfilled.'

Anna has my poem! The one I sent her in the autumn of '67! She has kept it all these years! She has remembered it!

'People are watched on street corners,
going happily to their own particular no-
    wheres,
knowing nothing of what we feel,
as we ride alone on wild horses of the
imagination
into an endless desert . . .'

'Stop!' I say. 'I know how it goes. I would never have guessed that you still had it.'

'Funny the things one keeps,' says Anna. 'I saw it in a university magazine years ago. A friend had it. I copied it out.'

'I had forgotten it was published,' I say. 'I

must have sent it to one of the student papers.'

She looks at me doubtfully.

'It's my poem, Anna! I wrote it!'

She seems confused, as if she doesn't know whether to believe me, as if uncertain whether yesterday's insanity has returned, or has never entirely dissipated.

'Are you sure?'

'Of course I'm sure.'

'So you must have gone to Southampton,' she says.

'Yes.'

'So did I.'

'No you didn't.'

She looks at me strangely again. 'Yes I did. What an odd thing to say, Matthew. I should know where I went to university.'

'You were going to Exeter.'

'When was I going to Exeter?'

'It's what you told me on Blackdown, that afternoon in 1967. That you were going to Exeter.'

I wonder now if I've remembered correctly. I must have done. I couldn't possibly have forgotten if Anna had said she was also going to Southampton.

'What afternoon on Blackdown? I wasn't in Somerset in '67.'

'Not this Blackdown. The other Blackdown.

The Surrey Blackdown.'

'I don't know what you're talking about.'

'It's my fault, Anna. It's all my fault. I should have mentioned it earlier. I thought it'd be fun to go on pretending.'

'Pretending what?'

'Pretending that we'd forgotten that we knew each other, back in '67. You were Anna Purdue then, of course. That July, when I came down to Lurgashall, where you lived, and Simon was playing cricket — do you remember Simon? — and we went off in my parents' Austin and spent the afternoon lying on Blackdown Hill, your special place. Lying on the hill and talking to each other.'

She continues to look puzzled.

'You've forgotten. I can see you've forgotten. That's all right. That's quite understandable. Why should you remember? It was only one afternoon, a long time ago. Anyway, that's when I fell in love with you, and you asked me to come to France with you the following week and I couldn't, and I was incredibly sorry about that, because I really wanted to come, but I didn't have any money. I thought it wouldn't matter because we'd be sure to see lots more of each other, but you never returned my phone calls, so I didn't see you again. Until Tate Modern.'

Anna gets up, moves her deckchair so that

she is now facing me. She fills her wine glass and pours a small amount into mine. I am breathing quite heavily.

'Matthew, it's all right. Everything's going to be all right.'

'If you say so, Anna.'

'Matthew, listen to me, please. Don't say anything. Just listen.' She leans towards me, touching my arm. 'My name is Anna Halfyard and always has been. I've never lived in Lurgashall, wherever that is, and I don't know any other Blackdown. I didn't go to France in 1967; I went to Italy. I didn't go to Exeter; I went to Southampton. I don't remember meeting you there. They were difficult years, so I may have done. I'm not the person you think I am. I'm sorry. I would like to be, for your sake. But I'm not. Do you understand that?'

I don't say anything. I can't say anything. I stare straight ahead of me, unblinking, unseeing. I'm not sure whether I believe her. She may be saying these things to get rid of me. There seems to be a choice. Either I believe myself or I believe Anna. Or perhaps she has forgotten certain things, quite a lot of things. Or perhaps I have.

In a contemporaneous universe, a phantom with the assumed name of Anna is saying something about going indoors to make supper. I rise from the deckchair, walk steadily to my car, start the engine, drive off. The phantom is waving frantically in the rear-view mirror.

13

In some beginning, too long ago for me to remember, the larva that was to become me pupated and took form. Chrysalis became imago. Imago became image, became self-image. A hybrid insect has half flown and half crawled through these years, blessed with the imagination to soar, cursed with puny wings. I want now to retract my legs like the wheels of a Jumbo jet, to fold my wings like summer clothes put away for winter. I want to roll my shell into a ball, a tight ball of soft material with an encasement of goo, and pretend that I am again the larva I once was and to become it again. I want to be a globule that someone will step on without noticing.

I'm on the road again. Not the A303. My car is on the road to Frome. Other cars pass it and their drivers are saying, 'That car is going to Frome.' They're not saying that, of course. Other drivers couldn't care less where this car is going, their eyes only on the car ahead and the prospects for overtaking. This car is going its own way. This driver is going somewhere, wherever somewhere is, on a road that leads to, well, anywhere. This driver is trying to select a route in the dark, not knowing his destination. This driver is dazzled by the bright lights of those who come towards him.

I couldn't remember what had happened to my bottle of whisky, so I stopped at an off-licence for another one. I had decided not to, but the imperative was too great. For many miles I wrestled with an overpowering desire for whisky. When I succumbed, I found that I no longer wanted it. The bottle sits beside me on the passenger seat, unopened, making small talk.

There is no hurry. I have the luxury of time and the luxury of money, the two things I once most wanted. I could drive for a hundred years and still have money to pay for the fuel. I could decide this instant that I will drive to Mongolia and do it. No one is stopping me. There is always more road. Always one more town to go to. Always another tank of petrol to get you there.

I've been thinking of a slim blonde girl, anorexic almost, with whom I had a one-night stand in my first year at university, trying to remember if her name was Anna too. I think it may have been. I can't be sure because I screwed a lot of slim blonde girls then. I can't remember the names of any of them. The only reason I think that one of them might have been called Anna is the coincidence of the name. Maybe that is why I screwed her in the first place, if I did. It's the coincidence I remember, not the girl. The song, not the singer.

Not that it matters now. I'm not going back to the Blackdown Hills. I'm done with Anna. She probably hopes that she's done with me. I don't know how our brains work, or our hearts, or if they work at all in any competent manner. I fancied the phantom Anna as much as the real Anna. I enjoyed her company just as much, found her just as stimulating. Whatever she thinks of me, it's not impossible that I could work myself back into her favour as a neighbour, not impossible that a year or two of certifiable sanity might reinstate me. But I'm not interested. She's a counterfeit and that's the end of the matter. I was looking for someone else.

I think I believe her, on the whole. I think she was probably telling the truth. In that case, I no longer believe myself. I'm not sure that I ever did.

The fact that this Anna is a fake means that the real Anna probably exists somewhere. I expect I could track her down if I wanted to. I've probably always been able to track her down, come to think of it. For some reason, I haven't. But I think I've had enough of chasing Annas for the moment.

I might end up going back to Judy. The direction in which the car has chosen to point itself is not inconsistent with Barnet as a destination. Nor is it inconsistent with many other destinations.

I'm going to turn off here. Here? Yes, here. This is the road I want. This is the one.

I wonder what Judy's doing now. I expect she's bearing up. People like Judy always bear up. It's a useful qualification, better than a bad degree from Southampton University. Judy has what is best described as phlegm, one of the four vital humours of ancient medicine: black bile, yellow bile, blood and phlegm. It makes me think of coughing up mucus, which is perhaps why I have such a low regard for it. I'm more of a bile person, myself.

I wonder if Judy has told the children. You'd think she has, not out of a need for sympathy, but to keep control of the narrative. That's all anyone does these days. It doesn't matter how crap the story, as long as you control the narrative. Could anything be more pathetic than spinning our own lives to ourselves? If Judy thinks I'm coming back, she may decide to say nothing for a while. She probably does think I'm coming back. She may be right.

This is not my favourite road. My brother died on it, what, nearly forty years ago. I'll be reaching the place in a mile or two. I'll recognize it as soon as I see it. I expect the tree is still there. I'll recognize the place even if it isn't. The tree will be taller now, of course. It wasn't that big at the time. I remember being surprised it was still standing after the crash. I put flowers by it. People didn't do that then, but I did. My dad said it was morbid. He cried when I did it, all the same.

We stood by the tree, my dad and mum and me, crying, trying to understand how it had happened. Alan was on his own, late at night, no seat belt. They weren't compulsory then. The weather had been fine. No other car was involved. No one witnessed the crash. There were no skid marks on the road. He hadn't been drinking. They examined the car and said there was nothing wrong with the brakes. He must have nodded off, Dad said, ploughed off the road at the bend, into the tree. The police didn't contradict that explanation. It became the accepted truth.

Alan was three years older than me. When I was about nineteen, three years before he died, he asked me if I'd ever felt like killing myself. It must have been around the time that I met Anna. Suicide was the last thing on my mind at the time. I had a future at the time.

I said no, I hadn't.

'I have,' said Alan. 'I think about it often.'

We talked about it for quite a long time. He had it all worked out. There was nothing unhappy about his life, nothing especially unhappy, nothing that didn't happen to anyone at some time or other. He knew already that life itself was unhappy. He was most worried about how Dad and Mum would feel about it. He didn't want them thinking it was their fault. It wasn't their fault, he said. It had nothing to do with them. It was him and how he was. Life and how it was. He said he would make it look like an accident.

I didn't tell anyone at the time. Alan didn't swear me to secrecy, so I could have done. I thought about telling Mum and Dad. There wasn't anyone else to tell that might do any good. I couldn't, not at nineteen. I couldn't tell my mum and dad that my brother was planning to top himself. Nothing happened for a long while after that. We were both wrapped up in our own lives. I can't say I forgot the conversation. I suppose I thought of it as being Alan's state of mind at one particular moment, an existential crisis that came and went. Until the 'accident'.

I still didn't mention it to Mum and Dad

when it happened, or later. What was the point? It could have been an accident. I didn't know that it wasn't. I still don't know. There is no proven connection between the event and a conversation three years earlier.

I sometimes wonder if they had any inkling. I don't think they did. And I wonder whether, if my own children felt like Alan did, I would have an inkling either. Probably not. I can tell if they seem to be happy or sad. That's about it. I've never talked to them much about their feelings. Judy does. At least, I imagine she does. I expect Judy would know if they were feeling really low, or at least have some instinct about it. I worry that these things are hereditary.

This is the place. I'll pull in here for a while. It hasn't changed much. The tree is still standing. There are one or two flowers growing at the foot of the trunk. I wonder if they could have seeded from the ones I left in 1970. I unscrew the cap of the whisky bottle and take a long, long drink.

I had an unremarkable career at school, running with the herd, pushing rebellion to the limit and not beyond it, fighting right up to the penultimate ditch. Just before my A-levels, I had a crisis. It occurred to me that I was the meat in the grinder of a huge sausage machine, churning away into oblivion. There was a choice, and this was the moment to make it or it would be too late. It was time to step off the conveyor belt.

I fudged the choice, as I always have. I told myself it was possible to be a hand-made sausage. I'm not sure now that it is. I have lived a life with my body on the conveyor belt, and my head hanging off it. That is no place to be. Time to make the choice now, I think. Time to submit to the grinder, or step off the conveyor belt altogether. Time to make a choice between different oblivions, different eternities.

The sandstorm conceals the desert. The smoke conceals the furnace. Nothing and no one are ever what they appear and the reality is always worse.

I think this is what I'll do.

I will drive towards Barnet. If I pass a late-night chemist before I get there, I will stop. I will buy as many paracetamol tablets as I'm allowed. I will swallow them with the rest of the loony pills I got in Bridgwater this afternoon, washed down with what remains of the whisky. If I don't pass a chemist, I will return to a house in Barnet and to a woman who lives there.

Supermarkets don't count. It has to be a chemist. There's no fun in backing odds-on favourites. I want to give myself a sporting chance. More of a chance than Alan gave himself.

I adored Alan. I looked up to him. He was way ahead of me, a lot more than three years. At twenty-five, he'd already worked out that life was not all it was cracked up to be.

I don't know why it has taken me so long.

We do hope that you have enjoyed reading this large print book.

Did you know that all of our titles are available for purchase?

We publish a wide range of high quality large print books including:
Romances, Mysteries, Classics
General Fiction
Non Fiction and Westerns

Special interest titles available in large print are:
The Little Oxford Dictionary
Music Book
Song Book
Hymn Book
Service Book

Also available from us courtesy of Oxford University Press:
Young Readers' Dictionary
(large print edition)
Young Readers' Thesaurus
(large print edition)

For further information or a free brochure, please contact us at:
Ulverscroft Large Print Books Ltd.,
The Green, Bradgate Road, Anstey,
Leicester, LE7 7FU, England.
Tel: (00 44) 0116 236 4325
Fax: (00 44) 0116 234 0205

THE BREAKING OF EGGS

Jim Powell

Feliks Zhukovski is a Pole in Paris — a hangover from another age. Estranged from his family by the Second World War, Feliks has given his life to Communism. As a travel guide to the old eastern bloc, his personal life is a resounding failure. Unfortunately for Feliks, it's 1991. Europe pulls back the Iron Curtain, taking away the certainties of his life. Potentially unemployed, Feliks is surprised to be selling his guide to an American firm, setting in motion life-changing events. Reunited with a brother he hasn't seen for fifty years, Feliks has hope of finding his mother and a long-lost love . . . after he finds a way through the smoke and mirrors of Europe's past. And the convictions on which he based his adult life.

THINGS WE HAVE IN COMMON

Tasha Kavanagh

The first time I saw you, you were standing at the edge of the playing field. You were looking down at your little brown straggly dog — but then you looked up, your mouth going slack as your eyes clocked her. Alice Taylor. I was no different. I used to catch myself gazing at the back of her head in class, at her silky fair hair swaying beneath her shoulder blades. If you'd glanced just once across the field, you'd have seen me standing in the middle on my own, looking straight at you. But you didn't. You only had eyes for Alice . . .